Praise for the Museum Mysteries by Sheila Connolly

"[A] clever, charming, and sophisticated caper. . . . A real page-turner!"

—Hank Phillippi Ryan,
award–winning author of *The Other Woman*

"Connolly's wonderful new series is a witty, engaging blend of history and mystery."

—Julie Hyzy,
author of the White House Chef Mysteries

Praise for the Orchard Mysteries

"There is a delightful charm to this small-town regional cozy . . . Connolly provides a fascinating whodunit filled with surprises."

—*The Mystery Gazette*

"A true cozy [with] a strong and feisty heroine, a perplexing murder, a personal dilemma, and a picturesque New England setting."

—*Gumshoe Review*

"The premise and plot are solid, and Meg seems a perfect fit for her role."

—*Publishers Weekly*

"A wonderful slice of life in a small town . . . The mystery is intelligent and has an interesting twist."

—*The Mystery Reader*

Books by Sheila Connolly

Museum Mysteries

Fundraising the Dead
Let's Play Dead
Fire Engine Dead
"Dead Letters"
Monument to the Dead
Razing the Dead
Privy to the Dead
Dead End Street
Digging Up History

Orchard Mysteries

One Bad Apple
Rotten to the Core
Red Delicious Death
A Killer Crop
Bitter Harvest
Sour Apples
"Called Home"
Golden Malicious
Picked to Die
A Gala Event
Seeds of Deception
A Late Frost
Nipped in the Bud

Victorian Village Mysteries

Murder at the Mansion

More Books by Sheila Connolly

County Cork Mysteries

Buried in a Bog
Scandal in Skibbereen
An Early Wake
A Turn for the Bad
Cruel Winter
Many a Twist
"Tied Up with a Bow"
The Lost Traveller

Relatively Dead Mysteries

Relatively Dead
Seeing the Dead
Defending the Dead
Watch for the Dead
Search for the Dead
Revealing the Dead

Glassblowing Mysteries
(Writing as Sarah Atwell)

Through a Glass, Deadly
Pane of Death
Snake in the Glass

Also Available

Reunion with Death
Once She Knew

Frances Eighmey
909 Hilldale Dr
Royal Oak, MI 48067

Digging
Up
History

Sheila Connolly

BEYOND THE PAGE
PUBLISHING

Digging Up History
Sheila Connolly
Copyright © 2019 by Sheila Connolly
Cover design and illustration by Dar Albert, Wicked Smart Designs

Beyond the Page Books
are published by
Beyond the Page Publishing
www.beyondthepagepub.com

ISBN: 978-1-950461-15-8

Digging
Up
History

Chapter One

I had almost succeeded in making the columns of numbers on the Society's estimated budget for the coming year add up when someone knocked on my door. I managed not to curse, but it wasn't easy: the annual board meeting was coming up fast, and I needed to get the spreadsheet worked out so I could write the usual scintillating prose to go with it—the sparkling language that would inspire the board members to whip out their checkbooks and write six-figure checks immediately. Well, I could hope, not that I could remember anything like that happening at any board meeting I'd attended since I'd joined the staff of the Society for the Preservation of Pennsylvania Antiquities nearly a decade earlier. Now I ran the place as president, after a few years as Director of Development, but it hadn't gotten any easier.

It was time for a break anyway. "Come in," I called out. Since my door was shut I couldn't see who was knocking.

The door opened slowly and I recognized Dylan Robertson, a grad student slash summer intern, the most recent in a long series of such interns. He managed to look both scared and excited, and he was gingerly clutching a paper-wrapped bundle. We'd hired him for the summer to catalogue and examine a collection of old books that had been left to the Society in the will of one of our long-term supporters. I didn't hold out high hopes that the collection would hide anything of great value, but Harriet Featherstone had been a lovely lady, and she'd wanted us to have something to remember her by.

I summoned up a smile. "Sit down, Dylan. I'm guessing you've found something interesting? Is that from the Featherstone collection?" I gestured toward his bundle.

I could swear that Dylan blushed. "I hope so, and yes. At least I think so. I've been doing some preliminary sorting and cleaning of the books, and making notes of what repairs might be needed, or if they're even worth repairing, and I found something unexpected. I think."

"Sounds interesting. Is that what you brought with you? Tell me about it. Oh, and please sit down—you're making me nervous standing there."

Dylan sat obediently. "You know about the collection, right?"

"Sort of. I knew Harriet, and she used to talk about the books her father had collected, and the ones that she had added, but I never saw any of them. I know she was proud of the collection, but that could mean anything. Have you made a quick pass through all the books, and can you tell me generally what's in the collection?"

"Sure. Mostly early-nineteenth-century books, leather-bound, not in the greatest condition. A few earlier Bibles that look like they've been well-used. The other books are what I'd guess you'd call serious—collections of sermons, some histories. Nothing frivolous like poetry or fiction. There are a lot of books—I can't guess how many yet because they're scattered all over the building. If you want to keep the collection together you're going to have to find some serious shelf space. Some of the books are more damaged than others, or are falling apart from age, even though it looks like Miss Featherstone took good care of them. You wanted me to give you an assessment of how much conservation would be needed, right?"

"Yes, I did. I do. And I'm hoping you can help out with that. I know you don't have much experience in physical conservation, but it could be a good learning experience for you. You could get a feel for the process with the less-valuable books—I'd call in someone to decide which those are. If you're willing, of course."

Dylan seemed to relax just a bit. "Sure—that would be great."

"Good," I said firmly. "So, what's that you're clutching?"

Dylan seemed surprised to find he was still holding it gently. "Well, this one has some particular problems. The cover's kind of falling apart, which is the only reason I noticed, but I thought I should let you look at it before I tried to do anything with it." He took off the acid-free paper wrapped around the book and held it out toward me.

I laid in on my desk, after clearing away a couple of stacks of financial records, and then I looked at it. It was fairly large, maybe eight inches by ten inches. The edges of the paper had been gilt once upon a time; the leather cover bore the remnants of a gold-stamped pattern. Once it might have been elegant, but now it was falling apart, the back cover dangling by a few threads. Either it had been well-loved or badly abused.

I opened it carefully to see what the text was. I was surprised: it appeared to be an early biography of some eighteenth-century person I'd never heard of, but the binding was clearly later, by maybe fifty years. Someone had cared enough to rebind the book? It didn't look particularly valuable, but I was no expert on antique books. Whoever had repaired it had done a poor job, since the cover was splitting apart. "What is it you wanted me to look at?"

"Inside the back cover," he said, then watched as I carefully pulled the layers of the cover apart. What I saw confirmed my guess that it had been rebound, because there were materials and techniques that hadn't been used until well after the book's original publication date. That much I knew. I was still puzzling over why Dylan had asked me to look at it until I noticed one of the layers of paper that had been used to reinforce the cover and its connection to the spine. Even I could tell that the paper was older than the book itself—it had probably been a handy piece of scrap paper that the bookbinder had salvaged from someplace else. While the paper was old, it was fairly heavy-weight and had survived well, apart from the various holes needed to anchor it to the binding. I hoped there wasn't glue involved, but the whole piece seemed to be slightly loose. I rummaged through one of my desk drawers and came up with a magnifier and looked more closely, and thought I saw handwriting on the paper. It too had faded, but it was definitely script of some sort written by a human hand, a letter whose lines were neatly aligned.

And illegible. I looked up at Dylan. "All right, there's a letter bound into the new cover for the book. Is that what you wanted me to see?"

"Yes. I've read about people finding all sorts of old letters or documents in books that have been repaired. Like it's recycling— why waste a perfectly good piece of paper? It probably didn't mean anything to whoever did it, but I thought I should clear it with you before I went any further."

"It's too hard to read in its current state to know who wrote it or to whom it was sent, but it might be possible to enhance it somehow to tell. Don't get your hopes up—it probably isn't from anyone important—but it could be interesting. Look, I know you're new to all of this, so I wouldn't ask you to do any delicate work on it, but I can call a friend or two to see what they think, and if they believe it's worth the time and effort, you can work with them. Is that all right?"

Dylan's face lit up. "That would be great! It'd be like getting to know a book from the inside out. Sure, I've read about how people assembled them and bound them, but it's not the same as actually handling one. If you don't mind, of course."

"You're here to learn, Dylan, and this is a good opportunity. And you're the one who found it. So if I can find someone with the right expertise, you have every right to be part of the restoration. If that's what we decide to do with it. Worst case, we could make it a stand-alone display so people could see how books were put together a couple of centuries ago. And you were right to bring it to me." I handed the book back to him. "See if there's a way to remove the letter without damaging the book, then let me know what you find out."

Dylan all but bounced out of his chair. "Thank you! You want me to go back to gathering and inventorying the collection now? Or should I handle the letter first?"

"If you can extract the letter easily, go ahead with that, but be careful—we don't know what we're looking at. When you finish that, go back to the collection so we can look at it as a whole and see where the letter might fit, and why someone cared enough to save it. Or maybe we'll find other rebound books. So go finish up the cataloguing, write up brief descriptions of each book, and we can go over it together. Does that work for you?"

"Oh, yes. It shouldn't take long—I'm about two-thirds of the way through it, and I'm trying to include whatever details I find."

"Good. Let me know when you're finished."

"Thank you, Ms. Pratt—er, Nell."

He pivoted and hurried out of my office, shutting the door behind him—leaving me staring at the battered book in front of me.

People who worked with antiques—items, buildings, whatever— held a small flickering hope in their heart that they might find something wonderful. Of course, we all believed that all old objects are wonderful, simply because they had survived for a long time in a chaotic world. But there are a few treasures lurking out there somewhere. Me, I'd started out as an English major and somehow drifted into raising money for institutions, but along the way I had caught the collecting bug. Luckily I could indulge it vicariously, since I worked in a building packed to the rafters with antique things, mostly books, but also some curious antique pieces that had been given to the Society by some long-dead donor and that we didn't know what to do with. Sometimes I fantasized that it was like a road map of history, except that all the pieces were scattered. That's one reason that Dylan was inventorying this new collection: to try to determine where it should be added to the Society's holdings. I didn't think that the collection itself was important enough to command its own space, but from my brief examination I thought it was worthy of being integrated, and that Harriet Featherstone should be honored for her contribution. I sometimes wondered whether she had simply inherited the whole lot from a deceased relative—Dylan had mentioned her father—how much of the collecting she had done herself, and whether she had enjoyed her own finds. She had been a lovely lady—and she'd also had a sharp mind and a good eye for collectibles.

I sighed. I'd have to think about who I could call, who might have any expertise in antique bookbinding. After I'd finished the financial reports.

· · ·

I arrived home almost on time, and when I opened the back door after parking, I was hit with a delightful blast of something that smelled wonderful. James had cooked! I didn't care what it was, as long as I didn't have to deal with it.

James and I were still kind of feeling our way through a relatively new relationship. Buying a house together had definitely kicked things up a notch, but I couldn't say that we'd established a basic routine. James is an FBI agent, so the demands of his job are very different from mine, but that gave us plenty to talk about (as long as his current assignment wasn't hush-hush). We'd worked together on more than one—what? *Case* sounded too formal, but there seemed to have been crimes involved. Still, I would say we worked well together.

"Anything interesting you can talk about?" I asked as he set a full plate in front of me, as well as a glass of wine.

He went back to the kitchen to retrieve his own meal. "Not much of anything going on. Didn't someone write a book called *Death Takes a Holiday*?"

"That was a movie, back in the thirties, I think, but I couldn't tell you who. But speaking of books, my summer intern Dylan found something interesting today. I was bored silly working on the Society's budget, so I let him explain it all to me."

"And this was?"

"I think I told you we received a bequest from one of our long-term members, who just died. I asked him to catalogue it and assess the individual volumes, see if they needed conservation and so on. He brought me an old book that was in bad shape, but the cover had already been replaced once. But that's not the interesting part. The newer cover was in bad shape, and apparently the bookbinder had kind of stuffed the new cover with whatever he could lay his hands on, to stiffen it up. From what little Dylan and I could see, there seems to be a letter inserted among the stuffing that looks older than the cover and maybe even the book itself."

"And what was it about?"

"That's what we don't know. We didn't want to rip it apart to find out, but there wasn't enough of it showing to make a guess. It may never be possible because it's so faded anyway. Which leads me to wonder if it's worth taking apart to see."

"Sounds like it should be rebound anyway, if the Society is planning to keep it."

"True. But I guess I'm naturally curious—I want to know what's in the letter."

"What would a conservator do?"

"I don't have a clue. That's the problem. I know the theory, but I've never done it, and I don't think this is a good way to start. I could call for outside help—I know a few people . . ."

"May I make a suggestion?"

"Of course. What?"

"This is on paper, right? With ink that looks brown now?"

"Yes," I said cautiously. "So?"

"It could be that the FBI lab would be able to help, without destroying the evidence, er, letter."

"Okay, I'm interested. But won't your office have a problem with you bringing something from the Society for them to analyze in your super-duper high-tech lab?"

"They could. But a few people owe me favors, and it wouldn't take long. And it wouldn't be invasive, which I believe matters to you."

"Well, yes—that's a good point. If it's a secret message from

George Washington, we'd all be drooling. If it's somebody's shopping list from 1800, not so much."

"You'll never know until you get a good look at it."

"True. Maybe I could bring it over to your office at lunch tomorrow, and we shall see what we shall see."

"Great. You doing the dishes or am I?"

"Is there dessert?" When James nodded in the affirmative, I said, "Then I'll do them. I'd like to eat dessert before I fall asleep."

Chapter Two

James and I did get some sleep before the sun came up. Our relationship was still kind of new, and some might say we had rushed into things, but neither of us was young, and we knew our own minds. We'd also been through some challenging times—like when I'd had to shoot someone to protect him—so we knew we could handle it. And I had to admit that it was kind of fun having an FBI agent on call as needed. It was surprising how many times I'd called him in to help with something odd happening at the Society—most people don't think of our library as a crime scene, but there had been at least one body since I'd been working there.

"Breakfast?" he mumbled into his pillow.

I rolled over to face him. "Is that a request or are you volunteering to make it?"

"I made dinner."

"That's right, you did. Do you have any early meetings or can I take my time?"

"No rush."

As I took a shower I reviewed my tasks for the day. The report to the board wasn't due until next week, and while I wasn't exactly finished with it, I knew I could get it done in time. I wasn't sure most of the board members would read it anyway, or more than the summary page. I'd asked Dylan to finish his initial survey of the Featherstone collection, and I hoped he could extricate the mystery letter bound into that one book (would there be more to be found in other books? I wondered). From what I'd seen of his work, he was careful, and I trusted he would come to me if that task was too much for him. I'd give him until lunch before nagging him about it; I had to admit I was curious to see what it turned out to be.

Then there was the question of who to ask to take a more skilled look at it, if it warranted further study. No way was I going to attempt to restore it, or even touch it, since I had next to no conservation experience. But I trusted James to handle it. I had to assume that any "evidence" presented to the FBI for analysis would be treated with kid gloves (or nowadays, latex). Besides, I wanted no more than a quick assessment from him, or his forensic people, so we could read it to find out if it was worth pursuing further.

I amused myself by imagining what it might be. Reluctantly I rejected General George Washington as the writer, not that there weren't plenty of documents in his own hand that had survived—he'd written a *lot* of letters in his lifetime. But he would still have been a household name back when the book had been rebound, so it seemed unlikely that the bookbinder hadn't noticed or cared. Maybe he'd hidden the letter deliberately . . .

Well, we wouldn't know who wrote it until we could read it, if that were ever possible, so I shouldn't get ahead of myself. If Washington had indeed written tens of thousands of letters, many of which had survived, I assumed many would not be extraordinarily valuable. But it might be worth a nice little piece of change, and the Society would have no trouble finding something worthy to do with it. Unless it was a bill for shoeing his horse, but if it was signed, even that prosaic item could be valuable.

James and I shared a leisurely breakfast—it was nice not to have any crises to attend to immediately—and I finally carried the few dishes to the sink. "Is it still okay if I bring the mystery letter over to your office at midday sometime?"

"Unless something unexpected comes up, sure. Don't expect too much—we've got only a skeleton team in the Philadelphia office. The main lab of course is in Quantico, and I don't think this merits their attention. But what you really want is simply to be able to read the handwriting and identify who wrote it and to whom, right?"

"That's a good start. It may be a receipt for a hat, for all I know, but I thought I should have it checked out. Of course, we museum people are always hoping for a big find, even though we know how rare they are. Maybe I should ask somebody on staff to check

Harriet's family tree—there might be someone up her family line who could have been the writer. Or the recipient."

"You're enjoying this, aren't you?" James said, smiling.

"I am. I'm happy to have something to do that doesn't consist of adding up columns of numbers, which never come out to as much as I'd hoped. And collecting and preserving is what we do at the Society. Sometimes I have to remind myself of that."

"Good point. Are we driving or taking the train?"

"I hate parking in the city when I don't have to. I vote for the train."

"Then I'll join you."

One nice thing about summer in Philadelphia is that so many people take vacations and head for "the Shore," which of course means New Jersey. That leaves the city much easier to get around in. But I still preferred taking the train—as long as the air-conditioning was working. When James drove, I actually had a chance to admire the scenery, take note of what had changed (things are always changing in the city), what had been knocked down, and what had been prettied up so owners and developers could demand a higher price. Still, it was a nice city to live in, although I admit I was enjoying a house in the burbs—particularly since James lived there too. And it was an easy walk from the house to the nearest train station, and once in town I could go all the way to the Society underground, so I didn't have to get wet when it rained. I figured it was the best of all worlds, if you liked cities.

I arrived on time and found Dylan hovering in the hallway outside my office. Not even my tireless administrative assistant had arrived yet, although she'd had to stay late a couple of times recently to work on those blasted budget pages, so I didn't begrudge her the time off. "Hey, Dylan," I greeted him as I opened my door. "Do I have time for a cup of coffee or have you made some amazing discovery?"

He looked a bit bewildered until he figured out I was joking. "Oh, I already made some coffee. Want me to bring you a cup?"

"If we're looking at antique paper items, we probably shouldn't put a cup of coffee anywhere near them. I'll walk with you to the break room and we can drink a cup there and you can explain what you've found."

"Sounds good to me," he said, and led the way to the far end of the hall. I was glad to see he wasn't carrying anything—like the Featherstone book—because I was scrupulous about not exposing any of our collections to contamination or just plain dirt.

Once we were settled, with reasonably fresh coffee, I said, "Okay, what've you got?"

Dylan was looking very pleased with himself. "Well, I stayed late last night because I was curious, but I didn't want to rush taking the binding apart. I looked up a few references on bookbinding and restoration, and I called one of my friends in my program, and then I very carefully took the thing apart. And I took pictures at each step, in case there's something I missed. I must have finished up around midnight, but I did manage to separate all the pieces of the binding."

"That sounds good. The letter came out intact? I mean, it was a letter, wasn't it? Not just a shopping list?"

"I think so," he said cautiously. "I can't say whether it was in lousy condition when it got bound into the book or whether something happened to it in the last two hundred years, but it's pretty much illegible. But, yes, it was a letter. Only I can't read it—it's too faded and stained. I *think* there's some kind of map on it, but it's just a jumble of lines which might be streets, so I won't swear to it."

"Any guesses?" I asked. I wasn't too upset because I knew I had James's lab in my back pocket.

Dylan shook his head. "Nope. I couldn't make out any words, though I think there are some, so for all I know it could be a map of the moon. Sorry."

"Don't be. I had a brainstorm. You know I'm involved with an FBI agent?" "Involved" was kind of an understatement, but our ongoing relationship wasn't exactly a secret, and I had to call it something. "There's a lab at the local headquarters. Not a big fancy one with a whole bunch of electronic super equipment, but one that can handle small projects. Plus some well-trained people who work there, and who James knows. He volunteered to ask one of them if they could take a look at the letter. He's been hanging out with me long enough to know how carefully this kind of thing has to be handled, so I trust him to keep an eye on the process. I told him I'd bring it over there today, assuming you had managed to retrieve it, and you did. You might want to go with him, if he can get you in—I don't think he knows a whole lot about eighteenth-century handwriting, so he might need an interpreter."

Dylan looked as though I'd handed him an early Christmas present. "That'd be great! I did see enough to say that it's not like a continuous letter. You know, with regular lines of text. Apart from the thing that might be a map, it's more like occasional words scattered around in no obvious order. That's all I could see. If I go, can I talk to the science guys? It might be useful to know what kind of chemicals or lights or whatever can work on paper without destroying it."

"We've got a few things here, but not enough for really serious work. We can clean things if we're careful, but anything delicate—which is most old documents—we usually send to a real expert. There's no shortage of those in Philadelphia. You must have noticed that already."

"Yeah, that's pretty clear. But I'm not worried about competition—I just like doing it. Handling the old things. Like little pieces of history, in my hand."

"Good for you!" I said enthusiastically, and realized how little I knew about Dylan. I might have chatted with him when he applied for the summer internship, but I had no idea where he was from or what his longer-term interests were. My bad. "So, are you going to show me what you've got?"

"Sure. Wish it was more. Should we go back to your office?"

"Follow me—and leave the coffee here!"

I led the way back to my office and sat behind the desk, moving what papers I'd left scattered on it. He waited until it was clear before he unwrapped his package—the same one as yesterday, only now it should be cleaner, I hoped—and laid out the letter, carefully protected by an acid-free sheet protector, and placed it gently on the surface.

I had to work hard not to laugh. I hadn't expected anything magnificent, but what I saw was a rectangle of paper that looked like it had been soaked in tea for years. It was interrupted by the occasional darker patch, which I assumed had once been handwriting. Plus a cluster of squiggles that must have been the hypothetical map Dylan had mentioned. It was disappointing, but I reminded myself that science had come a long way and sometimes it was possible to see things that were invisible to the naked eye. I hoped.

Dylan was watching me with a rueful smile on his face. "Doesn't look like much, does it?"

"No, but we're not done yet. This is just the first round. You've done a good job of removing it from the rest of the book without damaging it. Did you find anything else in the book cover?"

"No. Mainly it was what you'd expect to find on a two-century-old job—mostly padding. I think it's safe to say that nothing else there was as old as this piece of paper."

"Did you get any sense of whether it was concealed deliberately, or was used only because it was handy?"

"It was one layer of a bunch of layers—nothing special. I've saved all the pieces, and numbered them in order. I thought maybe some of the letters might have transferred themselves to another layer."

"Good thinking, Dylan. Let me give James a call and see when he'll be free. Or rather, his technicians—he's just introducing us. You don't have anything else on your calendar for today, do you?"

"Nothing that can't wait. I'm almost done cataloguing the Featherstone books, but they're a real hodgepodge. Did you know the lady?"

"Not well. She was already in her eighties when I started working here. She'd come to events that we held here, now and then, and she was kind enough to talk to everyone, including junior staff like me. I'll bet she had some great stories to tell, but I never had the time to listen to them all. I don't think she had a lot of money, although maybe she had come from a wealthy family. The book collection was all she left us, but nobody assumed they were rare or valuable. I think she just wanted to leave something for us to remember her by. Hang on while I call James."

I hit his speed-dial number, and he picked up quickly. "Hi, it's me. Dylan has separated the letter we talked about from the rest of the book. Is there a good time to stop by and deliver it? And I kind of promised him that he could see what your lab people do with it, if you don't mind."

"Now's fine, actually. Did he learn anything more about it?"

"No, it's basically illegible, but there's enough ink left to show that it had something on it. And squiggles—Dylan thinks it could be what's left of a map."

"Interesting. I'll meet you downstairs in, say, half an hour. That work for you?"

"Fine. See you soon!" I hung up and turned back to Dylan. "We're on, as soon as we can get there. Oh, maybe you shouldn't mention the FBI angle if you talk about this."

"Why not?"

"More than one reason, I guess—I can fill you in when we walk over. Nothing underhanded or illegal, and we're not paying for it, but I don't need the board members asking me why the first thought I had was to bring in the FBI. Okay?"

"Got it. I'll put the letter in something sturdier to carry it. Meet you downstairs."

Chapter Three

It was still cool and clear when Dylan and I set off for the FBI building. Another nice thing about Philadelphia: summer mornings. By noon it would be hot and sticky, but early enough it was very pleasant. I didn't often get a chance to do a little sightseeing, once I'd checked off Independence Hall and the Liberty Bell from my Must-See list, so it was a treat to stroll along and actually look at the city blocks.

"Did you grow up around here, Dylan?" I asked him.

"Nope, Delaware, although my folks used to make family visits to Philadelphia now and then."

"So you've done the obvious places. What about Valley Forge?"

"Not yet. I'm living in the city and I don't have a car, so I don't get out to the suburbs much. Is it worth the trip?"

"I thought so—but then, I only saw it a couple of years ago. If you're in the neighborhood for some reason, stop by and look around. It won't take you long. You must have seen Winterthur?"

"Sure. And the Brandywine Museum."

"I'm glad to hear that—I love that place. But how did you get interested in curatorship?"

"It always made me sad to see old things neglected and falling apart. And I'm sure I don't have to tell you that people don't often have the time or the skills to fix them."

"I know—sometimes it breaks my heart, what's being lost forever simply because of neglect. And I can't imagine living in a modern ticky-tacky house. I much prefer my Victorian. It takes work to keep it in good shape, but it's worth it."

I watched enough network television to know that the important FBI crime lab was in Virginia, but I also knew that many items were given a quick once-over in the Philadelphia building and a few other nearby locations. Since I didn't think we were dealing with something that contained an exotic new chemical, I thought we could

16

learn enough from the local lab to point us in the right direction.

Dylan and I took the scenic route, heading first toward the Delaware River from the Society, then turning north on Sixth Street until we reached the FBI building. James was sitting on a bench outside and seemed to be enjoying the sun—with his eyes closed.

"James? You taking a nap?"

James stood up quickly—not napping, apparently. "Hi, Nell. Just enjoying a moment of peace. This is Dylan?"

"Yes, sir." Dylan held out his hand, and he and James shook. "Thank you for agreeing to meet with us on such short notice, but we found the letter only yesterday, and I didn't want to do any further research until I knew what to look for. It shouldn't be handled too much—it's probably from the late eighteenth century, and it's kind of fragile."

"Interesting time to be in Philadelphia then," James commented. "Nell told me a little about the letter, or at least how it came into the Society's hands, but it sounds as though the survival of this letter was a happy accident, not deliberate."

"Probably, sir. But we won't know for sure until we can read some part of it. Preferably a name."

"Well, it shouldn't take long for our wizards to tell us whether anything is salvageable. This will probably be easy for them. And I promise we won't damage the letter. Ready?"

"Let's do it," I said with enthusiasm.

James took us inside the building, vouched for our honesty, dependability, yadda yadda, confirmed we were not carrying any weapons, made us leave our cell phones at the desk, and finally escorted us to the elevators. I sneaked a glance at Dylan, who looked mildly terrified at finding himself inside the FBI building. I knew his résumé hadn't included a criminal record, so I assumed he'd be safe enough.

We followed James down a couple of anonymous-looking halls until we reached something that looked like a lab. "Hi, Alice," he said to the white-coated staff member, who looked to be about Dylan's age. "These are the folks I told you about."

"Hi there!" Alice said brightly. Maybe she didn't get many visitors here in the back of beyond.

"Good to meet you, Alice," I said. "Thanks for helping us out. This shouldn't take you long. I admit I should know more about paper and things like that, but I'm an administrator, and I don't get to play with the scientific toys. Not that we have many."

"Hey, I'm glad I can help out your place. Will you give me a tour one of these days?"

"Of course! Anything in particular interest you?"

"Family history. I never knew my parents, and I don't know where to start."

"Don't worry—we can give you plenty to work with. You ready to start?"

"Sure. What've you got?"

I nodded at Dylan, who carefully extricated the letter from its sleeve and laid it on a flat work surface. "I found this bound into the binding of an early-nineteenth-century book that was recently given to the Society," he explained. "I could tell that it was earlier than either the book or its current binding, which was in poor condition. If I'm not overstepping, my guess was that the letter was just a random piece of padding that made the binding fit better, but I won't dismiss the idea that someone chose to hide it. The problem is, we can't read it. The ink has faded, almost disappeared, so we don't know if it was important or just a scrap of paper. We were hoping you could tell us more."

Alice smiled. "Gee, and here I thought you might give me a hard question. Just to check, the book was American? And the binding?"

Dylan replied, "The book was definitely American, and I think the new binding was too. It was not an important book, so I'm almost surprised that anyone had it rebound."

"Got it," Alice said. "Let me take a look."

I'd give Alice points for being thorough. She donned latex gloves, then turned on a high-intensity light over the work area and examined the paper, then she turned it over and looked at the other side. Then she found a magnifier and repeated the process. In all she took about five minutes to look at the single sheet before turning to us. "Dylan, I think you've got the basics right. Nell, what do you know about paper and inks in the later eighteenth century?"

"Not as much as I should, considering what my job is," I told her. "Can you read it?"

"In a minute. First let me tell you that it is pretty basic. It's probably written in what was called portable ink."

"What?" Dylan and I said in unison.

Alice smiled at our reaction. "This was not a piece of art, it was a simple letter, written with whatever was at hand, quite possibly during the Revolution, or at least thereabouts. Back then a lot of people, including soldiers, used a kind of powdered ink, made by grinding up a short list of ingredients. It was easy to carry around in a little packet, and all you had to do was add water, or even wine, and presto, you'd have ink you could write with. The main ingredient was oak gall."

"Which was what?" I asked. Why had I never known this?

"To be precise, oak gall is the common name for a large, round gall commonly found on many species of oak. It ranges in size from two to four centimeters in diameter and it's caused by chemicals injected into the tree's bark by the larvae of certain kinds of gall wasp in the family Cynipidae. Dry it, grind it up and sift out the lumps, and then with the addition of binding agents and a solvent, presto, you have ink, if you do it right. You can imagine even a soldier on a battlefield could manage that. You get a nice shiny black ink, although in some cases it can fade to brown—which is probably what you would see most often—or even fade entirely, which is what I'd bet you have here. Am I right in assuming I can't soak it in something to bring the writing out?"

"Please don't!" I said. "Maybe you could bring it back, but we don't know what we're dealing with here, and once it's gone, it's gone. Isn't there another way?"

"Sure. Ain't modern science grand? Because the oak gall contains iron, we can irradiate it harmlessly and the iron will react to the proper lighting, and we take a picture of what appears. Easy."

"Does it take long?" Dylan asked.

"Nah, just as long as it takes to find the right exposure. Watch."

Alice placed the letter on a ruled surface beneath a contraption I couldn't begin to identify. She turned the machine on and fiddled with a couple of dials until she was satisfied. Then she stepped back. "Come take a look," she told us.

Dylan and I all but fought for the first look. No longer was the page brown and blank, it had words on it, and the wavering lines that Dylan had thought he had seen. He'd been right: it was not a piece of correspondence with tidy sentences; the lines took up most of one edge of the paper, and there were various words and even numbers scattered among them. I had no idea what they meant, but at least they were visible now. Alice stepped forward, turned the page over, and repeated the process, and a few more details appeared on the second side. "Let me get some pictures of this. Step back, will you?"

Dylan and I stepped reluctantly away from the machine while Alice pushed some more buttons. "I'm putting these into a file, so you can take a flash drive back with you, but I'll print a few copies out for you so you can look at them now."

"That's great," I said, and meant it. "Do you have any idea about what's on the page?"

"Not a clue. It's not a puzzle, but I think you have to know something to make sense of what you see. I think we've got the date right—1770s or 1780s, but you'll have to figure out the rest yourselves. Is that all you need?"

"For now," I told her. "I'd love to bring half of the Society's collections over here so you could do this with all of them, but I guess that's not practical. Does this machine travel?"

"It could, but I wouldn't recommend it. You might want to buy one for the Society, though—could be useful."

"And how much would that cost us?"

Alice named a figure that took my breath away, but I didn't let that discourage me. I could see a practical use for it, and I was going to be talking to the board in a week's time—maybe I could interest one or more of them in supporting this marvelous toy.

But one step at a time. "Alice, I can't thank you enough. Whether or not this piece of paper is worth anything remains to be seen, but you've shown us a detail that could be valuable to us, and we've learned something new. Let me know when you want that behind-the-scenes tour."

"Will do, Nell. And I love talking about the process with newbies like you. It's kind of magic."

James, who had remained silent, apparently enjoying Dylan's and my wide-eyed excitement, stepped forward. "We've taken up enough of your time, Alice, but I think you've given us what we need. We'll get out of your hair now. Many thanks."

"Any time, Jimmy. Nice to meet you, Nell, Dylan. Dylan, don't forget your letter."

James—*Jimmy?*—led us back toward the elevators. Good thing he knew where he was going, because it appeared that both Dylan and I were still churning over what we'd seen and would have been lost without a guide. Once we were outside, we stopped again. "I've got to get back to work," James told us.

"Fine, go. And thanks—that was exactly what we were looking for. I'm guessing that Dylan and I are going to go back and lock ourselves into a room at the Society and study what we've got until it makes sense to us. I'll tell you later if we figure anything out."

"Yeah, thanks, Mr. uh, Agent Morrison. That was really great."

"Glad I could help. See you at home, Nell?"

"Yup."

James returned to the building. I took a deep breath. "Did

anything jump out at you?" I asked Dylan.

"Not really, but I didn't have time to really study it. Cool how turning on that light brought all the words out. Kinda like Alice said: magic."

"I agree. I don't know what we're looking for now, but we're already ahead of where we were when we started." We began walking slowly back toward the Society. "You know, it's almost like the precursor of the ballpoint pen. You carry this little packet of powder in your pocket, and when you need to write a letter you add water and you're ready to go."

"Assuming you happen to have a quill pen on you," Dylan added, grinning.

"Well, yes, there is that. Or you run around until you find a goose and whip up one of your own. Can't you just see a crowd of Continental soldiers running in circles trying to catch a goose so they could send a letter to Mom or a sweetheart?"

Dylan nodded. "Definitely a different perspective on that particular war. So, we're going to take a harder look at the images when we get back?"

"Might as well, while it's still fresh in our minds. But I don't want to get our hopes up. It still may be nothing more than an old piece of paper with squiggles on it."

Chapter Four

The heat had returned by the time Dylan and I started walking back to the Society, and I found myself wondering why this random piece of paper mattered to me. I knew that Dylan had been pleased by his find, and I had thought that studying it carefully would provide him with some solid experience. He was a good kid—careful, thoughtful, and committed to preserving the past, which was kind of rare in someone still in his twenties. I wanted to encourage him, but I didn't want him to get his hopes up that he'd found something special. It was a discarded piece of paper, used to thicken a book cover two hundred years earlier. How important could it be?

But I still hoped that there were happy surprises to be found in the Society's collections, and things that people had discarded a long time ago could still tell us a lot about the world at an earlier time.

Besides, I had to admit I was avoiding going back to those pesky columns of numbers. Yes, it took money to keep our place running—to keep the building standing without leaks, and with some climate control. And sometimes we might want to acquire new items that helped flesh out the existing collections and made the past a little more real to us all. And that took money too. The staff and I couldn't rely on the kindness of strangers to simply hand us what we wanted.

"You hungry, Dylan?" I asked. He'd been curiously silent since we'd started walking.

"What?" he said. "Oh, sorry, I wasn't paying attention. You want to pick up a sandwich or something?"

"Sounds good. I don't want to waste too much time, because I want to take another look at that letter. Which is kind of silly because it doesn't look like much, but we might as well be thorough. Besides, it'll give you some practice in the correct formatting of accession forms."

"Okay," he said amiably. "You want me to get the sandwiches while you go in?"

"I guess." It had been a pleasant morning, but I had work to do. "I'm not picky—just grab whatever looks good, and maybe a bottle of iced tea."

We'd reached the entrance to the Society, so I watched him head up Locust Street, then I sighed and walked in.

"Hi, Bob," I said. "Anything going on that I need to know about?"

He shook his head. "No, all quiet. Oh, but Marty Terwilliger is here, somewhere in the building. She asked for you, but when I told her you were out but would be back soon, she headed for the stacks. I'm sure she'll find you."

"Thanks, Bob," I said, and headed for the elevators.

Marty was someone who occupied a special niche at the Society. She'd been a board member for years, although she'd finally decided that board responsibilities were getting in the way of her own research. Her father had been involved too, for many years. And I counted her as a friend, after some of the unexpected events we'd been part of.

She knew more about the nuts and bolts of Philadelphia history than anybody else I'd met, but even I knew that research was never finished, so she was often to be found lurking somewhere in the stacks. It occurred to me that I might as well offer her a look at our mystery letter—maybe she'd see something that Dylan and I didn't. And she had probably known Harriet Featherstone since she was in diapers (Marty, not Harriet) and might be able to tell me something about how and where Harriet had put together her collection.

I made a beeline for my office, and I wasn't surprised to find Marty there waiting for me. "Where've you been?" she demanded when I walked in the door.

"At the FBI," I told her.

"Trouble?"

"Nope. Dylan found something interesting in one of the books that Harriet had collected—an old letter that had been bound into a newer cover—and he brought it to me. It's pretty much illegible, but I thought maybe the FBI lab could help us interpret it, and James was willing to get us in."

"And?"

"Well, it's more legible now, but I have no idea what it's about. Actually I would probably have gotten around to calling you—you know Philadelphia and its environs better than I do. Assuming, of course, it's from Philadelphia. Could be from Tibet for all I know. To be honest, I'm pretending it's part of Dylan's training, but the reality is I'm avoiding writing the board report for next week. But it's kind of fun. Like a puzzle. Was there something you wanted to talk to me about?"

"Not really, although I guess we haven't talked for a while. Things good with James?"

"Just fine, thanks. We love the house—it's not too near the city, but not too far." Marty had helped us move in and knew the house well. "What about you? Have you heard from Eliot lately?"

Eliot was a delicate subject at the moment. Marty had been a highly independent single woman for years now, but then out of the blue she'd gotten involved with Eliot Miller, a professor at the University of Pennsylvania, and things had been warming up nicely between them until Eliot left for a year's sabbatical. His letters, emails and phone calls were few and far between these days.

"No," she said, and did not elaborate. "I'm sort of between projects, and I got bored. So this is where I headed. I guess it's kind of my home away from home, and I always find something new. What's this letter thing Dylan found?"

"That's just it—we don't know. It looks late eighteenth century, but I'm no expert. The ink has mostly disappeared, but one of the FBI techs managed to make it visible again. But that didn't help much—it looks like a few random lines, with some words and numbers scattered around. Maybe it was a page from a child's exercise book, for all I know. But the FBI has some really cool machines—I think we could do a lot with them here, if only we could afford them."

"You just need to find the right donor. Who is not me, please."

"You've done more than your share, Marty."

Dylan appeared at the door, laden with plastic bags. "Oh, hi, Ms. Terwilliger. Don't let me interrupt you. Nell wanted some lunch. There's plenty if you want some too."

"Sounds good to me—I've been in the stacks for a couple of hours. Nell tells me you found something interesting?"

I interrupted. "Let's hold off on discussing that until we can actually look at it. In the meantime, why don't you tell us about Harriet Featherstone and her family while we eat?"

Marty rifled through the bags of food before answering. "Another old Philadelphia family. I went to school with a nephew of hers, back in the dark ages. You already know she never married, but she did love history, and she loved collecting—which two things are not the same. Did you ever see her house?"

"No, I'm sorry to say," I told her. "By the time I came along here, she wasn't entertaining much. I take it you saw it?"

"On and off for years. She had interesting tastes. I seem to remember a pair of Japanese silk shoes intended for bound feet, next to a Tiffany desk set, on top of an Early American table. Eclectic, to say the least, but she liked it that way. And I liked her—she was an original."

"How did the Society end up with her book collection?"

"You're a library, aren't you? Where else would you put books?" Marty said tartly, as she bit into a sandwich.

"Anything interesting among them that you recall?"

Marty shrugged. "Not really. She bought things she liked, and she didn't care if they were valuable. But she didn't believe in wasting money either, so she wouldn't have bought anything magnificent. Just things she enjoyed."

"Did she spend much time at the Society when she was younger?"

"I think so. My father knew her fairly well. I remember catching glimpses of her here when I was a teenager, but I didn't know her well."

"So now we have this book—which Dylan disassembled when he saw the letter—"

Dylan interrupted. "The binding was falling apart. I tried not to do any damage, but I thought maybe the letter was important."

"Don't worry about it. What do you think the letter is?" Marty asked.

"I think it's a map. Something somebody sketched out in a hurry, because it's anything but finished. I haven't had time to figure out what was written on it—mostly short notes, not anything like a description. But it's definitely old, and hand-drawn, not printed. I couldn't see it well enough at the lab to decipher anything more, but Alice at the FBI gave us a flash drive with the images, so we can enlarge it if we want. If you think it's worth it," he ended dubiously.

Marty briskly bundled up her lunch wrapping and tossed it into the trash basket. "Why not? You never know what you're going to find. Let's finish eating and go take a look."

It didn't take long for us to finish eating, and then we adjourned to the pitifully small area in the back of the building where we did what restoration we could. At least it had good light, both from the large windows (which could be covered to prevent overexposure to sun) and from the lights suspended overhead. There were work surfaces available, and they were reasonably clean. We all dutifully washed our hands to get rid of any sandwich residue, and then Dylan pulled out the folder and removed the letter, laying it in the middle of the work surface. Marty didn't say anything, but leaned over it and studied it—or what there was of it. Then she walked around the cabinet and looked at it from other directions. She stopped opposite where she had begun. "This is the bottom end, here."

Dylan and I trotted around to stand next to her. It didn't look particularly different to me, but I was happy to bow to Marty's superior experience.

After a few more moments of studying it, Marty turned to Dylan. "You were right—it's a map. Not much to it, but there wasn't much to the city when it was sketched. It was never meant to be pretty—it was for information only."

"Marty, are you saying it's part of Philadelphia? You recognize it?"

"I'm pretty sure I do. Hang on a second." She picked up the case she was carrying and found a map inside. Then she laid it next to our mystery letter. "This is an official map of Philadelphia, circa 1780. You two should recognize the general outlines of the city, but only the colored parts existed at that date. In case you haven't figured it out, that's the Delaware River on the right."

"And those little jagged things are the docks?" I was beginning to get excited: even I could see what she meant.

"Got it in one, Nell. A lot of them, weren't there? It was an easily navigable river. Along the water there were lots of warehouses, and then street or streets behind that were where the merchants lived. At least for a while—the city grew fast, so the people with money moved west pretty early. Hey, you got a projector that will enlarge what we're looking at?"

"We've got the flash drive with the image. You want it bigger than just computer-screen size?"

"I want to check something. Maybe there's more written there than we think."

"I'll set it up," Dylan said quickly, and moved to another work surface, this one against the wall. Above it was a blank area about three feet square. He pulled out some sort of enlarger, then set it up and inserted the flash drive and turned the whole thing on. Marty moved over to stand by him.

I had the feeling she saw what she had expected to see. "What is it, Marty?"

"This is probably from around 1770. You can see that most of the first generation of houses is still standing. And there are numbers next to many of the houses—hard to see without enlarging it. We should try to find a city directory for the era and see which was which."

I made a wild guess. "Marty, did one of your ancestors live in one of those early houses?"

"He did. James Terwilliger. Inherited money, oversaw the family shipping business, and was a general in the Revolution. Though there were lots of generals, he was one of the good ones. I knew that house."

"Marty, you're not two hundred years old!" I protested.

"I said most of the houses were long gone. Some were kind of forgotten, squeezed between later buildings or remodeled so you couldn't tell how old they were. Could be there are still remnants there, unless developers have gone crazy putting in expensive condos with river views. When I was a kid, maybe eight or ten, me and my cousins used to snoop around there. Without telling our parents, of course. There were old foundations, and cellars, and even some tunnels connecting the houses, out of sight. And maybe even tunnels linking them to the waterfront. Look, I was young and I had no idea what I was looking at, but it was a great place to play and make up stories. I do remember there were a lot of things down there that I couldn't identify. I mean, I know what a barrel looks like, and I think there were bottles there, but it was dark and damp and hard to see. And we only played down there for two or three years—after that our parents made us pretend we were civilized, so I guess we never went back. I don't know how much survived." Marty looked wistful.

But there was one important question I wanted answered. "Marty, why would anyone draw a map of that block? At that particular time? This letter of ours doesn't look like a kid's drawing."

Marty finally tore her eyes away from the image on the wall, and she looked at me. "I don't know, but I'd love to find out."

Chapter Five

Dylan was staring at Marty as though she was some sort of magician. I had forgotten that he'd only met her once or twice, and there was a lot about her that he didn't know. And a lot that he could learn from her as well. Marty knew pretty much everything there was to know about Philadelphia, both past and present. She also knew who was related to whom, going back a dozen generations. She was never obnoxious or pretentious about it—she simply had a good memory and a lot of curiosity.

So now she was curious about why anybody would make a rudimentary sketch of riverside property in Philadelphia circa (did I dare say it?) the Revolutionary War. I knew what most moderately educated people who'd attended an American school (public or private) knew about that era, combined with what I'd picked up working in the heart of the city at an institution that specialized in history. The more I had learned, the more I had come to realize that our modern textbooks and curriculum focused mainly on the "cute" stories, probably because they were easier to remember, but which didn't really give a full sense to the time. Was that good or bad? Most likely most people in the country had heard of the Liberty Bell, only a few blocks from where I now sat. But did they know why it mattered? Did they care, after they'd learned what and where and how old it was and passed the standardized test?

I had to shake my head to clear it. We were talking about a raggedy piece of paper that had been stuck in a book for two centuries, not some significant piece of history. Marty said it showed some early streets in the city. Okay, fine—they had been real once, and many were still there. So what?

"Earth to Nell?" Marty said nearly in my ear, and I jumped.

"Sorry, Marty. I was trying to figure out why this piece of paper exists, and if it means anything. I'm inclined to say no, save that people can find interesting things where they least expect them. Do you have a different idea?"

"Maybe. Give me some time to think about it."

"While you're thinking, let me ask you this: are you interested in it because of fond childhood memories of playing in those streets—or cellars or tunnels or whatever—all those years ago?"

"Does that make it more or less important?" she shot back.

"It could certainly be important to you, but to other people?" I countered.

Marty got a faraway look in her eyes. "I know how we can find out," she said.

I was almost afraid to ask how, but I could make some educated guesses. "Marty, do you have reason to believe that some or all of what was shown on that map is still there? Not buried under a parking lot or a hotel?"

"Yes, but not for much longer."

"Why do you say that? Global warming will make the river flood an entire block of that end of the city?"

"It might, but that's not what I was thinking."

"So?" I noticed Dylan was silently watching the two of us as though we were playing singles tennis.

"You're right about waterfront development. For a while nobody would touch the properties there, not because of historic significance or even the highway, but because the underlying ground was just too wet, since it's right next to the river. But technology has improved, and there are some eager developers who think there's a way to drain the land and keep it dry. And they're starting to poke around in the dirt there, make some test holes and such—right about there." Marty pointed to one intersection in the middle of the projected map.

"Marty, why on earth do you know this?" I asked. "You live at the other end of town."

"Yes, but I know the developer. I went to school with his sister."

"And this connection means what?"

"That if we want to see what's there, we can. And now is the perfect time."

I wasn't sure what I felt. Marty thought we should go poking around in eighteenth-century mud looking for . . . what? "Isn't there some city historical organization that keeps an eye on things like that? I can never remember which group is responsible for what."

"Of course there is. You've met some of the members, and they come to Society events. And if you don't know them, you should. I'm sure they wouldn't mind us looking at the site, as long as we signed the right waivers or something. And don't walk off with any artifacts we find."

I wondered briefly if the Society's insurance covered senior staff falling into a large hole in the ground, historic or not. I sighed. "So what are you suggesting we do? I assume you do mean 'we'?"

"Of course. It should be interesting, and you'll learn something. And so will you, Dylan. Bet you didn't know that studying book repair and cataloguing involved wading through muck." She grinned at him.

He returned her smile—it looked like he was getting into the idea. "Not exactly, but it sounds like fun."

"Okay, okay," I said. "When are you thinking of making this expedition?"

"First I need to contact my friend and clear it with him. Relax, you two—the project has barely begun, so it won't be too messy yet. Nell, I'm surprised you haven't heard anything about it."

"Why would I? I don't even know what 'it' is."

"Okay, here's the short version. Barnaby Construction Group wants to build an apartment building on Second Street, and they've got the city permits lined up but they haven't broken ground. Like I just told you, that's where General James Terwilliger built himself a nice house after the Revolution. But he didn't stay long because the city was moving west fast. I told you some of my cousins and I used to poke around what was left of the old places down there, but even that hasn't been possible for a long time. Makes me feel old, I guess, since I remember so many changes in the city. Anyway, various other structures were built in those blocks, but the most recent was an asphalt parking lot. Not the best use of a historic site, but I didn't have any standing to stop it, and the city wasn't quite sure which agency could intervene for historical purposes. Anyway, the Barnaby Group saw an opportunity to purchase the land, then get rid of the parking lot and build something better. I've seen some sketches and I think he's got a good plan. I mean, it's not going to be a glass and steel tower. I hear he's got some solid investors lined up, and they want to get the shell assembled during the summer."

"Marty, what's all this got to do with the Society, and us?"

"Because that's exactly the spot that the letter or map or whatever it is shows, back when there wasn't much of anything there except docks and shipbuilders. Maybe we can find something that would make a nice article for the *Inquirer* or a magazine, and everybody would benefit."

I had to admit it wasn't a bad idea, especially since Marty had the connections to make it happen. "Okay, I see your point. And I should know more about the city—the parts *under* the streets and parking lots. But I've still got the pesky board reports to finish."

Marty waved a dismissive hand. "Don't worry, they'll wait for you. And the meeting isn't until next week, right?"

"Correct. If I'm late with them, will you write me an excuse?"

"Sure. And if we're lucky we'll have something to show them."

"Then I guess I'm for it. When were you thinking?"

"Today. The weather's good, and I know Barney—he's the head of the company—will be poking around there. He's like a kid with a new toy. It wouldn't surprise me to find that he's going to buy one of the apartments himself—preferably one with a river view."

"But do we have to get muddy today? I'm not exactly dressed for it."

"Call it reconnoitering. We're scoping out the site. And I want to know what the timeline will be and what he's planning. Let me give him a call." Marty bounced out of her chair and walked into the hallway, punching buttons on her cell phone.

Dylan and I looked at each other. "Marty Terwilliger is a force of nature, and she knows everything there is to know about Philadelphia," I told him.

"I've heard people talking about her—only good things, of course—but I haven't seen much of her myself. But I like the idea of this project. If there ever is a publication, would I get my name on it?"

"Sure, why not? As long as you mention the Society. You found the letter, so you get first claim. And who knows what else we'll find? Did you ever read John Cotter's book *The Buried Past*? He and a bunch of other historians explored what people in that general area left behind in the privies of the city and other unexpected places. It's worth reading, if you have the time, and it tells you a lot about life here during an earlier era. Anyway, this project might be a bit cleaner. But definitely historic."

Marty returned quickly. "He's there now, and he says come on over. Nell, you up for that?"

"I guess. Beats getting any real work done. And there's history involved in there somewhere."

I realized Marty was looking at my feet. "What?"

"You got any better shoes for walking? Because this could be muddy."

"Sure, I've got a pair of running shoes I wear when I try to catch the train."

"Put 'em on," she ordered. I complied.

It was a short walk to Second Street. It didn't seem long to me since I'd last strolled in that area, but it seemed a lot of things had changed: there were new projects scattered all over, in various states of construction, from piles of dirt to final touches. "You know, Marty, I really don't get out enough. There's just so much history here."

"And a lot of it is covered up with all sorts of things. Like parking lots."

"At least we can hope that whatever's under them has survived."

"Maybe. I've been told that they even left a lot of early stuff under I-95 when they were building that—cheaper and easier than digging it all out. But do people care? I mean, they can Google pretty historic maps and they'll see a lot more than messy holes in the ground."

"And what do you want people to do with all this evidence of the past?"

"Save as much of it as they can. Oh, you and I both know the city can't go around building museums on every corner. But if you know what you're looking for, you can read Philadelphia's history like a book, from the bottom up. Somebody should care."

Dylan had remained silent so far, so I turned to him. "What do you think, Dylan? You're the next generation, and you're already working on antique items. Is all this worth saving? If it all morphs into apartments and stores and maybe some places to eat lunch, will anybody notice?"

"Maybe if they know it's there, or was. Hey, I started digging up small-town dumps when I was about ten. I loved finding old stuff, even when I didn't know what it was or how long it had been there. That's what got me interested."

"Good for you!" Marty proclaimed. "Like the way my cousin Nate and I used to poke around in old cellars. You find the oddest things." She slowed, then stopped, looking around. "We're here. And there's Barney." She waved vigorously, but instead of coming over to join us on the sidewalk, he gestured toward us to join him in the middle of a plot the size of a city block, scraped down to dirt. Marty didn't think twice about it, and I followed more slowly.

"Hey, Barney," Marty said. "Thanks for letting us see what you're doing here. Do you know Nell?"

Barney, a sturdy middle-aged man wearing a grubby baseball cap, said, "I don't believe we've met, but I've heard your name from a number of people. Did Marty insist you come along with her?"

"Not exactly, Barney. We found something at the Society, and I told Marty about it, and she said we needed to look at this lot. One of her ancestors lived near here, right?"

"Sure did, but it was a long time ago. His house is long gone, and I don't have any idea who thought putting in a parking lot was a good idea. So we've stripped that off and started digging so we can figure out what we need to do about foundations, but then we kind of stumbled over something that may hold us up a bit. Want to see?"

"Sure. Was there something under the parking lot?"

"I'd guess *somethings*, plural. Come take a look—and try not to fall in a hole."

Marty and I followed Barney toward the center of the lot, with Dylan tagging along behind. The ground looked kind of churned up—at least it was dry, but it was kind of uneven, like people had been attacking it with shovels. But not big earthmovers, I noticed.

"Look over there," Barney said, waving broadly. "What do you see?"

I edged closer to the place he had pointed to and peered into the dip there. And peered again, because I was having trouble believing what I was seeing. "Are those . . . bones?"

"Yup," Barney said, beaming.

"Human?"

"Sure are. Lots of them. Looks like we've stumbled on an old cemetery. Every time we stick a shovel in the ground, we find more. And coffins too, or at least pieces of some."

"Didn't anybody know this was here? Your construction guys, or even the city?"

"Nope. I checked all the city records when I was planning this project, and there was no mention of a cemetery here. At least, not that we've found. Hey, you're the lady at the history place—you've got a better chance of finding out what's going on here than most of us."

"I guess so. Marty? You know anything?"

Marty seemed distracted, but finally she focused on me. "Not really. Not yet. I might remember something from when I was a kid, but I'm going to have to think about it. Maybe I thought it was a big secret, so I never mentioned it to the rest of the family. It's been a long time. Barney, what're you going to do?"

"I have to hold up work until we can figure out what's going on here. I'm pretty sure you'd skin me alive if I just went back to excavating without getting somebody's approval, now that you know about it. Maybe you could tell me what agency I should be talking to."

"I'll make some phone calls," Marty said quickly. "Nell, you have any ideas?"

"I don't usually deal with properties, but I can certainly check our files. Dylan, you want to help? Knowing who's who in the local historical community could be useful to you."

"I wouldn't miss it. I want to know what happened here."

"What's your timeline, Barney?" Marty asked.

"Oh, we're already behind schedule. But if I can score some points for preserving the city's important history, it can't hurt."

She turned to me. "Nell, you in?"

"Why not? Tomorrow's Saturday, right? I can check the obvious references, and then maybe we'll know how to go forward. And who we should talk to."

"Great. Barney, let's meet here in the morning and pool our information. If you've got the deeds to this place, bring 'em along. Somebody must know something."

"I sure hope so," Barney said. "See you tomorrow. Nice meeting you, Nell."

Chapter Six

We didn't talk much on the way back to the Society. I checked my watch and was surprised to find that it was only midafternoon, but I wasn't sure what I wanted to do. I really didn't want to go back to crunching numbers, but I didn't feel I had enough time to start looking through the collections of city maps and the like to try and find out more about that piece of ground we'd just seen.

Barney seemed like an okay guy, or at least not one who would ignore whatever building regulations existed and plow ahead with his building, skeletons be damned. He might not want to make public the fact that they were there, because no doubt there were potential buyers who would prefer not to live on top of a cemetery, even one that had not been used for a long time. Would I? I liked cemeteries, mainly because of the genealogy information they held, but I wasn't sure that living on one would feel right.

But Barney now knew that Marty would be keeping an eye on things and wouldn't let him get away with anything shady. And he probably knew that if he stayed on her good side, she could help smooth the road with the right city agencies and figure out what to do.

When we reached my office, I turned to Dylan. "You want to take a shot at finding whatever history is attached to that plot? Barney more or less said it had to be a cemetery, given its size, and not just a random burial of a couple of people, so there should be some public information about it. And it had to date back to the eighteenth century, because that's where the city was then." Or it could be later, because I was no expert at determining the age of bodily remains, but why confuse Dylan now?

"Sure," Dylan said quickly. "This is really interesting. And how do you misplace an entire cemetery full of people? I want to know more. Listen, do you want me to come along tomorrow? I can bring a camera and stuff."

"Sure—another set of eyes would help. But please don't talk about this to anyone else for now—we have no idea what the legal status of the land is, or what's going on below the surface. Marty and I will let you know when it's all right to talk about it publicly. But do keep notes on what you learn—you may get a publication out of it yet."

"Thanks, Nell. You want to meet here or at the, uh, apartment site?"

"Let's meet at the site. Say at ten? That work for you, Marty?"

Marty's head jerked up, as if she was surprised to hear her name. "What? Oh, sure, we can meet there. Assuming the weather co-operates."

"See you then," Dylan said, and headed toward the stacks, brimming with youthful energy.

Marty still looked a bit dazed. "Are you all right, Marty?" I asked.

"Yes. And no." She shut the office door and flopped onto the settee against the wall—one of the perks of my elevated status. "You have time to talk?"

"Of course. Is something wrong?"

"I don't know. There are a lot of things I haven't even thought about for years. Since I was young, in fact. I think I always knew there was a cemetery near John Terwilliger's house, but I never went looking for it or saw it. If I had to guess, I'd say back then the cemetery lot was covered with grass, without any buildings on it, but I never paid any attention to it. Then of course they built I-95 right in that area. I wasn't even driving then, so we didn't visit that part of town much."

I wondered if Marty was going to make a point, and she didn't keep me waiting. "I told you that when I was a kid—ten or even younger—my cousins and I used to snoop around that part of town. It's a wonder we didn't get hurt, but I guess we were lucky. And it's not like we were looking for anything, like treasure or something— we were just having a good time. Nobody gave much thought to that part of town, back then. I think we picked it only because our families kept talking about which of the ancestors had lived around there, way back."

"But you never noticed any remnants of the cemetery?" I asked.

"No. Or, not exactly. Don't rush me, Nell. I'm trying to piece together some pretty ancient memories, and I certainly wasn't a historian when I was ten, just a curious kid. But there was one thing . . . I forgot about it, probably on purpose, because it was creepy. We found a body."

I hadn't exactly expected to hear that from Marty. "What do you mean? Overflow from the cemetery? Some homeless person who crawled down there to die and nobody ever noticed?"

"Somewhere between those two, I'd guess, in hindsight. Look, you never saw those houses when they were standing. You know they were close to the river. And, yes, there were some tunnels or other ways of accessing some of the houses, if you didn't want anyone to see you."

"Like smugglers, you mean?"

"Yes, or maybe spies. And you know that General Washington spent a lot of time around there, for years. Maybe he sneaked in and out occasionally."

"Marty, you're driving me crazy. Okay, so you and your cousins—I'll assume most of them were male—played hide-and-seek in the ruins of eighteenth-century houses near the waterfront, and there was a cemetery nearby. The one you say you didn't know existed. And you found a body in the basement or maybe sub-basement of one of those houses, and you never mentioned it to any responsible grown-up. Have I got it right so far?"

"Close enough. It was our secret. We didn't even tell our friends—at least, I didn't. If we had, they probably would all have gone down there and started pawing through the ruins. Look, I don't know if that house or any part of it is still there. Maybe it was razed like the cemetery. I wouldn't have known if anyone had found a body there—I wasn't exactly reading daily newspapers then. But before you bite my head off, I want to say two things. One, it wasn't close to that cemetery Barney found, so it wasn't like it was a body they crammed in at the edge when they were running out of room. Didn't have a coffin either. Two, it's exactly the location that map Dylan found shows. Maybe that letter wasn't just a piece of wastepaper. Maybe somebody was sending a message, and that's why my dead man ended up there, dead, or somebody wanted to be able to find him later. I can't begin to guess who or why, but the place and maybe the time are right. It was an old skeleton even then—not much flesh left, as I remember."

"Did you ever go back?"

Marty shook her head. "No. I think we'd all seen enough. And like I said, we never talked about it, and kind of went on with our lives."

I thought about it for maybe thirty seconds. Marty was not the kind of person to make up something like this, and she probably hadn't been at age ten either. "Marty, do you want to find out if that body is still there? If anybody ever discovered it? And why somebody thought it worth making a map of? If you don't say anything now, I doubt Barney is going to stumble over it, because it's not exactly in his building lot. You may not get another chance."

She looked me in the eye then. "Yes. I do. I know a lot more now, about the city and its history, than I did back then, and this just doesn't sit right. Particularly the letter. Somebody wanted to know where the body was. And maybe there was something more there that we didn't find. And now we have the perfect opportunity—and excuse—to snoop around and find out. Maybe it's all long gone, and we can forget about it again. But I want to know."

I could understand that. As part of the historical community in Philadelphia, I was still horrified at how many treasures from the past had been discarded altogether, or stolen by tourists who saw no reason why they shouldn't palm a cool—and free—souvenir. How much of the past had been permanently lost? So that people could have parking spaces? And now purely by accident an old letter and map had landed in our laps, and we had a pretty good idea of the location it showed. We had every right to check it out. If we found nothing, nothing was lost, and Dylan could file the letter away under "Anonymous Manuscript, late eighteenth century."

"Then let's look for it," I said firmly. "Barney's already agreed to meet us there tomorrow morning. Right now we don't know whether the particular place we want to find is still intact in any way or disappeared a long time ago, but that should be easy enough to check, either by just looking at what's there or by checking city records. Or maybe Barney knows something—maybe he bought it, or maybe he found he couldn't buy it for some reason. Do you trust him?"

"About ninety percent, I think," Marty said dubiously. "He's not really into history, so I'd guess that if he found something under there, he'd be happy to hand it over to one or another museum. Or ask me who would want to have it. Unless, of course, it turned out to be a pirate's chest of gold doubloons, being guarded by that skeleton I remember, which he could probably find some use for. But let's not tell him what we're up to until we know a bit more. As far as he knows, we're just curious about the cemetery."

"And we're going to wait to get in touch with any of the city agencies until we know more?" I asked.

"I'd say yes. If we find something, we'll tell them next week. That should give us time to collect information. If there is any."

"Okay!" I said, slapping my desktop. "We have a plan. Tomorrow we'll hunt in the dirt for a cemetery that shouldn't be there, and a body that may not be there. Sounds like how I spend most of my time. I will dress appropriately for dirty work. Should we bring any tools? Dylan will have his camera."

"A shovel wouldn't hurt, or maybe some brushes. We don't want to damage anything. Just in case."

"Can James come? You know he's trustworthy. Besides, he can do the heavy shoveling."

Marty grinned. "I always feel better with an officer of the law handy. Although I doubt we'll come upon anything that relates to his business."

"I'm going to assume that current laws about reporting finding a body to the police will not hold in this case. But I'm sure James will tell us if they do. And from what you've said, that person, whoever he was, has been dead a very long time."

"Wonder if we're related?" Marty said, more to herself than to me.

"It wouldn't surprise me."

My cell phone rang then: James. Speak of the devil. I hadn't realized how late it had gotten. "Hi," I answered. "Where are you? I mean, downstairs waiting for me so we can go home, or still at your office mired in work?"

"The first one. Can you leave now?"

"Yes—it's been pretty quiet here today. I'll be down in five." I ended the call, then looked at Marty. "I would have asked you to join us for dinner, but I want to kick this around with James first. There's probably nothing we need to worry about, apart from telling some-one there's another body, in addition to however many there are in the cemetery. If it is a cemetery, and not just a dumping ground. And if the other body is still there. If we don't find it, that's the end of the story. If somebody says, 'I'll swing by and pick it up,' I guess we don't have to worry about legalities, beyond maybe a short report. You can decide how much you want to tell people about the first time you found him—it was a 'him,' right?"

"There are a lot of 'ifs' here. If I didn't imagine the whole thing. If he's still there. If the building he was under is still there. If there's any evidence of who he was and what he was doing there. And if we tell the authorities about the letter, if the answer to all those other 'ifs' is yes."

"Why wouldn't we? It's evidence, if they feel the need to ID the person. Or they may not even bother, if the person has been dead a century or two—a lot of work for them, with no predictable results."

"True. Look, you go meet James, and you can hash all this over at dinner. Me, I want to go home and think about it. Like I told you, it's been a long time, and memories are tricky things. Maybe it was just a heap of old rags in a dark corner, and we jumped to some conclusions before we ran. Remember how young we were."

"All possible. I'll see what James has to say. Then we all rendezvous at the construction site in the morning and see what we find. And if it really was a cemetery that the city forgot, you can make sure that Barney lets the right people know."

Marty stood up. "Sounds like a plan. I'll walk down with you. If we need to do research, I can come back here tomorrow."

The front door was still open. James had opted to wait outside, and with such nice weather I couldn't blame him. "Hey," I said. I was still kind of reluctant to get into a romantic clinch in front of the museum/library that I ran, but that doesn't mean I wasn't tempted.

"Hello, you," he said. With remarkable restraint. Then he noticed Marty behind me, and his tone became more formal. "Hello, Martha. We haven't seen you for a while."

"James," she replied. "You may be seeing a bit more of me. I'll let Nell explain. Ten o'clock?" she said to me.

"Yes. Tomorrow."

Marty turned on her heel and headed for her own home. James looked at me. "What was that all about?"

"I'll explain over dinner. No, not on the train—I don't want other people to overhear."

"Okay. This should be interesting."

"I think it will be."

Chapter Seven

We talked about nothing in particular as we walked toward the train station across from City Hall. I was still a bit distracted by what Marty and I had seen earlier, but James didn't insist on conversation. I wasn't sure what to tell him anyway. As far as I knew, Marty and I weren't looking at a crime. All the possible bodies on Barney's building site had been dead a very long time. Probably their great-grandchildren were dead too by now. There was no killer to find, and nobody to prosecute. What the city decided to do with the bulk of the bodies wasn't my problem, although I certainly was curious about what had happened that had left them there, hidden for all these years.

We caught our train with time to spare and found seats easily. As I had expected, a lot of people with jobs were probably headed "down the Shore" at the moment. And for once the air-conditioning in the train car was working.

"Is there anything in the house to eat?" I asked when we were about halfway home.

"I won't swear to it. Take-out? Chinese? Or Thai?"

"Thai," I said decisively. "Wine?"

"Plenty of that," James replied.

We stopped at a hole-in-the-wall restaurant a few blocks from our house and emerged with a couple of bags of food that smelled wonderful. Another five minutes' walk and we were home. I dumped my bag of food in the kitchen and said, "I'm going to go put on something grubby, and then I'll explain what Marty and I were doing today while we eat."

When I returned to the kitchen, James had already distributed plates and utensils around the kitchen table and filled two glasses with wine. "You are amazing," I said, dropping into a chair.

"Are you ready to talk now?" he asked.

"And let me add you are phenomenally patient. Yes. But this may take a while. You don't have anything else you need to do, do you? No significant baseball game to watch?"

"You have my full attention," James said, helping himself to some kind of noodle dish.

"Well, I told you about Dylan finding that letter, and then we all went over to your lab and made it readable. Then Dylan and I went back to the Society and we ran into Marty, who after looking at the letter decided it might be part of an old map of the city, and she thought she knew the area it showed and wanted us—that included Dylan—to go look at it immediately." And then I described the site, and the plans for it . . . and the bones her developer friend had found. "And then Marty remembered something that she'd seen a long time ago in the same area, when she was a kid, and wondered if and how that fit with what we'd seen today, but she wanted to think about it, maybe decide if she'd only imagined it. So we went back to the Society and talked about it, and we're planning to go back tomorrow morning and take a better look at the construction site. She knows the contractor, so there's no problem with getting in."

"What do you think you're looking at?" James asked when I ran out of breath.

"Most likely a cemetery. I gather there are a lot of abandoned ones in the city, particularly in that part of it. There's a website that shows where many of them were located, which I never knew about until now. I can't figure out if builders a century or more back were in a hurry, since the city was growing so fast, or just lazy."

"What was it that Martha remembered?"

"Keep in mind, she was only about ten years old." I took a long swallow of my wine and held out my glass for a refill. "She thinks she remembers seeing a body in a nearby ruined house. Her ancestors came from right around there, a couple of centuries ago, and she and her cousins kind of hung out there, exploring, when they could get away with it. I gather finding what they thought was a skeleton freaked them out. They never told anyone else, and they didn't go back."

"She doesn't think it was part of the hypothetical cemetery?" James asked.

"It's about a half a block away from that. Of course, there could be a lot more bodies in between, but the one she remembers didn't have a coffin or a stone to go with it, and it seemed to be the only one in that particular place, and pretty much hidden under an old building. And then there's the map. Which, by the way, has some sort of writing on it, as you know, but we didn't have time to study it carefully."

"So you and Marty and Dylan decided to go back tomorrow and snoop some more?"

"Yes. Look, Marty's developer friend is the one who discovered there are some bones buried there, right where he wants to build. He didn't know how many, but he said he'd checked the available records and gotten all the necessary construction permits from the city and nothing like a cemetery had turned up. Marty says he's an honest guy. He'll be there tomorrow, mostly because he's curious now."

"What's your goal?"

"Well, at a minimum we could discover that it was a forgotten cemetery, which might have some news value, at least to the Society, if we claim we found it. I don't know if Barney has thought that far ahead. But we've got his permission to look, and Marty knows who works for the city, who she should call, if this turns out to be anything. And, of course, since we're there sort of officially—at the request of the property owner—she wants to check out the place where she found the body in the old days. Which could easily be long gone now."

"If that body existed, and not just as a kid's fantasy, it could be just about anyone. Male?"

"Yes. Or at least, she didn't mention a dress. And she wasn't really sure how old it was. Could be eighteenth or nineteenth century, or even later, but not real recent. Listen, did we once talk about whether all unidentified bodies had to be reported to someone in the city? The police, maybe?"

"The medical examiner—it's his responsibility."

"And how long does Philadelphia keep records of unidentified bodies?"

"I think it's safe to say, not long enough for your needs. Why is this important to you?"

"In part because I'm encouraging Dylan's initiative and curiosity, and he seems to be having fun with it—he really does like history. But mostly for Marty's sake, I guess. The fact that this map or whatever has survived this long, and was somehow preserved in a book, makes me wonder if it's important. Yes, I know it's a real leap of faith to think that it points to a body that may or may not exist and hasn't been mentioned for years, but it's possible, isn't it?" I stopped suddenly, hit by a new thought. "You know, this book was part of a collection donated to the Society by a longtime member who passed away recently, and who knows how long she or her family had it before that. This was not the only book she left us. I should ask Dylan to check out the rest of them—maybe there's more information hidden away in the bindings. And I want to find out some more details about who Harriet Featherstone was, and who her ancestors were, and where they lived. Maybe this was a long-lost relative of hers."

James was smiling again. "What?" I demanded.

"Don't take this the wrong way, but I think you just want an excuse to get out of your building and walk around the city, since the weather's so nice."

I smiled back at him. "Well, yes, just a bit. But this is related to history, sort of, and I'm mentoring new staff members, and helping Marty, who's been an incredible supporter of the Society for most of her adult life. So if anybody complains I'll tell them all that and more."

"I'm not arguing. Do you want me to come with you tomorrow?"

Had he read my mind? "Well, there are bodies involved . . . but only if you want to. I'm sure the three of us can manage."

"I'm happy to come. There's a lot I don't know about Philadelphia, especially the really old parts. And, as you say, there are bodies involved. You might need some protection."

• • •

The next morning we were running late—I never seemed to get around to memorizing the train schedule, since we often drove in—and I was struggling to pick out clothes that would withstand heavy labor but wouldn't make me look like a homeless person, in case somebody important wandered by. Or a photographer from the *Inquirer* on a slow news weekend. In the end we decided to drive. After we'd parked (not always easy near Independence Hall on a summer Saturday), I climbed out of the car and waved at Marty and Dylan, standing next to Barney in the middle of the large dirt patch. I leaned toward James and asked quietly, "You don't know Barney, do you?" When he shook his head I added, "How do you want me to introduce you?"

"I guess boyfriend would be a bit silly. Just give him my name, okay? We're not investigating him or his project."

When we were nearer the small group, I called out, "Good morning! Your work crew's not here today, Barney?"

Barney gave me a smile a bit less enthusiastic than the one the day before. "Hi, Nell. No, I thought we should figure out what's going on under the dirt before we tore it up any more."

"Has anybody learned anything new? Don't feel bad if you haven't had time to do any research since yesterday. Now we're all starting on the same page. Any new thoughts, Barney?"

"Not really. After you guys left yesterday I poked around a little more—carefully!—and it seemed like there were bones everywhere I looked. Martha here has been telling me that we ought to try to figure out where the boundaries are. I mean, is it just a bunch of bones dumped in the middle of the lot, or do they cover the whole site? Because if it's the latter, this is more likely to be a cemetery. Though for the life of me I can't figure out why somebody simply forgot about it and covered it over. Looks like there's room for a lot of people here."

"I agree. Marty, did you have any brainstorms?"

Marty looked somewhere between nervous and depressed. "I made some bigger prints of that letter, so we can see the details better. Not that there are many. But there wasn't much around this few blocks around 1800 anyway. I need some time to look at more of the old maps."

"But you recognize the shoreline of the river, right?"

Marty finally came up with a smile. "Might have been all those big docks that gave it away. So, Barney, where do you want to start?"

"I'd say with the corner nearest Market Street—that was the busier end back then because it was an important street. Then work our way back toward Arch Street. If you find any more bones, give a shout but don't mess with it. And the kid here can take pictures of anything interesting. Just don't start digging until we know what's what."

I looked at the others. "How do you want to do this? Solo or in pairs?"

"I vote for pairs," Marty said quickly. "In case one person falls over a skeleton. And no souvenir hunting. We're supposed to be responsible people. And you run the Society, Nell, so that would be doubly bad."

"You want to come with me?"

"No, you take James along. I want to be alone to face my memories. Think we'll have seen enough by lunchtime?"

"For a first pass, I'd say yes," I told her. "And I want to eat lunch at the Reading Terminal."

"Why am I not surprised?" Marty said, smiling. "Let's go!" She turned and walked briskly toward the street side, while James and I went in a different direction.

We spread out along one edge of the empty-looking lot and started walking slowly, peering at our feet. I gave a fleeting thought to the people walking around the neighborhood, oblivious to what we were looking for. Probably just as well, because if they knew they'd run screaming or come looking for relics of their own.

It took me a while before I stopped flinching at the sight of a grinning skull at my feet—after the first twenty or so examples. Unless there had been a major battle here—and I probably would have heard about that, given the sheer numbers of people involved—this had to be a cemetery, not just a random dumping ground.

"Kind of overwhelming, isn't it?" James said softly. "I've seen what look like fragments of wooden coffins, although the pieces are pretty small."

"It is that," I replied. "I'm still boggled by how any group could completely forget about this many bodies, when they seem to have been properly buried. Can you extrapolate how many there might be here, based on what we've covered so far?"

"I can give you a rough guess, no more. I'd say at least two, maybe three hundred."

"Wow. I seem to remember that as of 1800 Philadelphia had about forty thousand inhabitants. What do you make of it?"

"I haven't decided. From a modern forensic perspective, I note that there are no obvious wounds—like bullet holes—among any of the dead, at least the ones we can see in the top layer. There could have been a plague—I'm not up on medical history here. A mix of male and female. If there had been a big fire, I would expect to see more obvious damage to the remains. Am I missing anything obvious?"

"Apart from the sheer number of bodies? The only other question I can think of is, can you tell over how long a period these bodies were buried? I don't expect you to get the right year, but was it over twenty years or a hundred and twenty?"

"Hard to say, without more careful examination, and I don't think the FBI is going to want to step up for that. Maybe we can cut a deal with the medical examiner. Or you can scrounge up a willing volunteer."

"Maybe Dylan has some archeology friends," I said dubiously. "They might think exploring this would be fun."

"Worth thinking about. How much more do you want to finish today?"

"I think we've determined that this must have been a cemetery, given how large the space is and how many bones we've seen. The Society has the resources to figure out which one. And we're far from experts at analyzing old bones. You've eyeballed them and ruled out death by fire, but most of the other options are still on the table. We've already figured out that we need some expert advice. So I'd say we could call it quits at any time. You see the rest of our crew?"

James stood up and stretched, then checked out the lot. "Dylan's over there. I don't see Marty or Barney. Damn, we should have brought water bottles or something."

"I'd put money on it that Marty's trying to track down the old house where she thinks she saw the skeleton. Of course, it could be a grocery store by now, or a phone center."

"You remember enough of the map to guess where that one would be?"

"Only that it was on the east side of the lot. That's the side toward the river. Want to head over that way and check?"

"Might as well," James said, his tone resigned.

"That way, then." I pointed. But we'd only made it halfway there when Marty emerged from what looked like a hole in the ground and waved at us.

"Hey, guys, you've got to see this."

So Marty had in fact found something. I hoped it was what she was looking for, but I wasn't going to hold my breath.

Chapter Eight

As we approached Marty, I tried to read her expression. As far as I could tell she looked excited, and I felt a small tickle of excitement myself. Sitting in my nice office it was easy to forget that we were literally sitting on history all the time in the city. Now here we were standing in the middle of it. Maybe Marty had found nothing more exciting than a 1900 trash heap, but that would still be over a century old and therefore history.

"What've you got?" I said when I was in earshot.

"Well, if nothing else I've proved that I wasn't crazy. This is the right place, though it seems a lot smaller than it used to."

"You know whose building this was?" I asked as I studied the bits and pieces of the half-ruined building. It looked to me as though half the original building had long since fallen or been removed, leaving the back end embedded in somewhat later construction. The older part wasn't visible from the street, and if you weren't looking for it, you might never notice it. It looked like a lot of old Philadelphia buildings I had seen, although this one was in a better neighborhood. It was surprising to me that any part of it had survived.

The foundation, or what I could see of it, appeared to be brick, minus most of its mortar. A few feet higher there was wood siding on the exterior, but most of it was concealed by layers of various kinds of later siding, including asbestos tiles. Higher still there were window sashes, but the glass was long gone and most of the openings had plywood nailed over them. I didn't think I'd ever known when plywood was invented, but I was pretty sure it was less than a century ago. Did someone still own this property, or did some city agency spend their time running around boarding up old buildings for safety reasons?

"Could you get in?" I asked Marty.

"I haven't tried yet. There's a big hole in the foundation at the side, but I don't know if it's the same one I used before—and I was a bit smaller then. But it's big enough for a human."

"Is the hole old or recent?" James asked.

"I didn't study it. I don't think it's antique, but it's probably older than last week," Marty told him.

"If it's an old hole, wouldn't everything and anything have gotten in?" I asked. "You know—rain, snow, rodents, homeless people and so on. And wouldn't that have weakened the foundation?"

"Probably. What are you saying, Nell? That it is a newish hole and somebody's been poking around in there?"

"Marty, I don't know. I'm just tossing out questions. Or maybe somebody else knew about it the same way you did. Have you talked with your cousins lately?"

"About this? No, of course not. It's ancient history, and they're really not interested in the past."

"And you don't know if anyone else who knew the hole—and whatever's inside—was here?"

"Why would I?"

James spoke up. "Are you seriously thinking of going in?"

Marty turned to face him squarely. "Well, yes, actually. Why? You want to go first?"

"I'm not sure anyone should go now. We have no idea how stable the structure is, and it could end up falling on your head. We need to shore it up and be cautious about it. Where's Barney?"

"I haven't seen him since we started. Dylan was with him. Have you seen him?"

"Not lately. Wait—there's Dylan. We can ask him if he's seen him," I said, spotting Dylan approaching from Market Street. He was carrying a plastic bag with what looked like bottles in it. Smart boy: he'd found us some water.

Dylan held up the bag. "Hey, guys, I got some water for us. What's going on?"

"Marty's found her hole. You know where Barney is?"

"I told him I was going for something to drink and then I left. He's not here?"

"We haven't seen him lately. Maybe there was something else he needed to do," I told him.

"He didn't mention it to me," Marty said in a sulky tone.

"You need him for something?" Dylan asked.

"As I said, Marty found the hole she remembered and of course she's itching to crawl into it," I said. "James sensibly pointed out that the building could fall on her head. The foundation seems to be original, with a lot of later patches, and I know I wouldn't trust it. We were going to ask Barney if he had any way to shore it up enough for us to peek inside."

"Sounds risky," Dylan commented. "Maybe we should wait until we can make sure it's stable? Or, wait—I can go in," he said eagerly. "I'm the smallest of all of you. And I can take pictures so I don't have to go all the way in—just enough to see if there's anything there. Don't worry—I'd back out fast if it started creaking."

I could almost see the battle going on in Marty's head. On the one hand, she really wanted to see what was in the hole. On the other, she was a responsible adult and didn't want to put young Dylan at risk. "James, what do you think?" Marty asked plaintively.

"I think you're crazy. But I guess I understand. Dylan's right— he's the only one small enough to fit easily at the moment. Let me keep hold of his ankles, and if anything starts happening I'll drag him back out fast."

Great—now this wild-goose chase was putting James at risk too. I didn't like any part of this. "Not to threaten your manly pride, but are you sure you're up to this?"

He grinned crookedly at me. "I always wanted to go on a treasure hunt. Look, if the building's been standing here at least most of this past century, if not longer, it will probably survive another day if Dylan worms his way in to take a few pictures. And of course I'll be careful. I've survived at the FBI this long, haven't I?"

I wondered if Marty would pay for his funeral. "Go, you two, before I have a hissy fit." Having been given permission for this ridiculous effort, James looked almost as young as Dylan. Me, I tried to remember any first aid I knew, but I was pretty sure that none of it included rescuing people from collapsing antique buildings. I didn't dare look at Marty.

Dylan went first, laying down on his stomach at the entrance to the hole in the wall. "Hand me the camera, will you?" Marty leapt to hand it to him. When Dylan had wormed about half his body into the hole, James lay down behind him and grabbed his ankles.

"Take it slow, will you?" James called out to him. "And don't go too far in. Just check out a few feet ahead of you."

"Got it," Dylan called out, his voice muffled. I could see his feet inching forward, and when he was about five feet inside, he stopped. "Wow," he said almost reverently.

"What?" Marty called out.

"I'll get pictures," Dylan replied, and we could see intermittent flashes as he took picture after picture. Gradually the brightness of the flash dimmed, and I wondered if he was running out of battery power. "Coming out," he called to James behind him, and James started wriggling backward carefully. It took a couple of minutes for Dylan to extricate himself, and then he stood up and brushed off the dust of ages, while the rest of us watched silently. I was beginning to think Marty was going to explode when Dylan dusted off the camera lens, scrolled through some pictures, and handed it to Marty. "Thought you ought to get the first look."

Marty took the camera carefully and looked at the viewing screen. For a long moment she was silent, then she finally said, "Wow. I was right. We were all so scared we just left—fast. But there is definitely a body, or at least what's left of one. Needs a bit of cleaning up." She turned to me and handed me the camera. "Take a look."

I looked. "It's a pretty murky shot, but that certainly looks like a body to me."

James held out his hand, and I passed the camera to him. He studied the photos with care before saying, "You're both right. I hate to admit it, but I thought you were hallucinating, Marty. My apologies. Now we have a body, and that's only what we can see from a snapshot."

"What do we do now?" I demanded.

"I don't have a clue."

We didn't have to decide right away, because a pair of street cops appeared and one demanded, "What's going on?" Nice to know the local police were on the job. I shuddered to think what they made of us—three middle-aged people plus one younger one, all covered with mud, dust, and I didn't want to guess what else. In the middle of an otherwise empty vacant lot—if you didn't count the scattered skeletons. I wondered if the policemen had noticed any of the randomly distributed skulls as they had made their way toward us.

Luckily James stepped forward, because I had no idea what to say. I hoped he had a clue. He reached into his back pocket and pulled out his FBI ID and flashed it. "I'm James Morrison of the Philadelphia office of the Federal Bureau of Investigation. This is Eleanor Pratt, president of the Society for the Preservation of Pennsylvania Antiquities, and Martha Terwilliger, a former board member of the Society. We're here because we were informed by the property developer that there might be human bodies on the site, and he wasn't sure of their age and wanted our assessment."

"Bodies, huh?" the older police officer said. "Like a few? Recent?"

I figured James would prefer that Marty and I kept our mouths shut for the moment, so I let him answer. "No, probably a couple of hundred. Plus one more under that building there."

"Hundreds, eh?" the officer said sarcastically. "Where are they?"

James pointed. "Just walk around what used to be the parking lot there. They're hard to miss."

"You folk been drinking? Smoking weed?"

James replied in a sharper tone, "Just take a look."

The two officers exchanged glances, and then the younger one trotted over to the main lot. Clearly neither one had believed us, not that I blamed them, so it was kind of fun watching the younger officer stop suddenly and stare at something at his feet. I had a pretty good idea what it was. Then he moved forward, more cautiously, and stopped again. And again. Finally he returned to where we were waiting, placing his feet carefully. "Uh, Sarge, they weren't kidding. There are lots of bones over there."

"Huh," the sergeant said, and I could almost hear the gears turning in his head as he tried to figure out what to do next. I doubted the Philadelphia police force had found an entire lot full of skeletons very often.

Luckily James stepped in. "Sergeant, I suggest that you tell your superior and then call the medical examiner. I think we have a lot to sort out here."

"No kidding," the sergeant said. "So how the hell did you all stumble onto this?"

I decided I should say something now. "Ms. Terwilliger knows the developer, who called her when he had cleared the asphalt off this lot. He knows she knows local history and wanted her to take a look and maybe tell him who to contact next."

"Where's he?"

"We don't know. He met us here earlier. We were all here just getting an idea of how many bodies there were, and he apparently left while we were looking. We haven't seen him for a while. He did say he's gotten all the appropriate construction permits for this property, so apparently there's no official record of all these bodies. That we or the city know of, anyway." I exchanged glances with Marty, who was curiously silent—in shock, maybe?—before adding, "We might want to get someone who knows urban archeology to take a look at this site, before anyone starts carting the skeletons away. This is clearly a historic site and should be handled as such."

Sarge didn't look very happy about my suggestion, but he hadn't looked happy before I made it. "You know anybody like that?"

"I can find someone," I said firmly. I was pretty sure I could, with Marty's and Dylan's help, and I would bet that some eager archeologist would jump at the chance to investigate this. Then I added, "Maybe you should put some sort of guard on this place. I bet a lot of crazy tourists would like to pick up an unusual souvenir from their trip to Philadelphia, and I'm sure the word will get out pretty fast."

Poor Sarge was looking more and more bewildered. "I'm going to call headquarters and see what they say." He turned and walked away, nearly tripping over a skull.

While he talked on the phone, the rest of us stared at each other. "Well, this is interesting," I commented. "What happens next? James, you're the expert on bodies."

"Not quite as old as these. Or as numerous. Marty, I'm glad you pointed out the gentleman under the house."

Marty looked defensive. "I'm not hiding him—although he's been pretty well hidden for quite a while. But I want a historian to look at him before the police or the ME drag him away.

"Dylan, I'm grateful to you for thinking of taking the pictures. It's good to know that I saw what I thought I saw, all those years ago. You know, I think I know a lot about Philadelphia, and particularly this end of town, but I'll admit all that we've seen today surprises me. I'm going to have to figure out a strategy."

"We all do," I said. "Look, I'm exhausted and hungry and filthy. All I want is to go home and have some wine and take a shower and eat something, not necessarily in that order. You two are welcome to join us."

Both Marty and Dylan declined—they both looked about as tired as I felt, and I knew Marty had a lot to think about.

"I've got to figure out who to call to make sure we don't lose whatever evidence there is. And I need to call Barney—wonder why he hasn't come back? And the head of the Revolutionary War museum. And of course there's a lot of information at the Society."

I wasn't sure if she was talking to us or to herself. "We've got two days' worth of time to do research, since we're not open Monday. And I wouldn't call the official folk tomorrow, since that's Sunday. Who's going to be the public spokesperson for this?"

"I'd vote for spokespeople, plural," James said. "I can handle the investigative side, unless some major case comes up at the FBI, but Marty knows a lot more about the situation, and the possible history of the site. She's right—this should be handled carefully."

"Then I vote that we go to our respective homes and rendezvous at the Society tomorrow. And see if you can track down Barney, okay, Marty? He really needs to know what's going on. And if this makes it to the news, he may want to have a say in how to present it. It is at least under his management, if he doesn't own it outright."

"Got it," Marty said. "I'll call you in the morning and we can decide when to meet. And thank you all for agreeing to what I was afraid would be a wild-goose chase."

And so we went our separate ways for the evening. I had no idea what would come next.

Chapter Nine

James and I walked back to the car in silence. Marty and Dylan had each gone their own way, without comment. Like Marty, I needed time to think.

I had been an English major in college and then a fund-raiser. I knew a lot of general things about American history, and even about Philadelphia history, but I was not prepared to deal with what we had just found. Marty was better equipped, but she had no official standing with the Society now that she was no longer on the board, although unofficially she was an invaluable resource. James represented law enforcement, although I wasn't sure we needed that. Clearly none of us had killed all those people. But there they all were, and whether or not we had a legal obligation to establish who they were and how they'd been left there for so long, they were now a piece of Philadelphia history and deserved some attention, and I didn't want to think of the police or the medical examiner's office bundling them up and dumping them into a pit somewhere, or worse, burning the bones.

And then there was the man in the hole. Being skittish kids, Marty and her cousins had probably caught sight of a skeleton and turned and run. And it had been a long time ago.

I wished I had thought to ask Dylan to send copies of the photographs he had taken to our home computers, so we could enlarge them and see if there was more detail.

"You're quiet," James said when we got to the car.

"I'm thinking."

"I thought you might be excited. This could be an interesting find, and maybe even a feather in the cap for the Society."

"I haven't thought that far. I'm still stuck on why anybody would simply forget about a couple of hundred buried skeletons. In a small town I could understand it—and aren't there some towns that were deliberately flooded for dams and the cemeteries were left behind?—

but this was a big city in that era, and that part of the city was its heart back then. How do you forget a cemetery that takes up an entire city block?"

"That I can't answer. But you may be the best person to find out."

"I'm not sure that was on my résumé when I applied for the job."

We drove in silence for a mile or two. "I'm glad you were with us," I told James. "It never occurred to me that the police would show up, not that they didn't have every right to, because we certainly could have been trespassers or scavengers. Either way, it was good to have a man with a badge on our side. I feel almost sorry for those police—they couldn't have been expecting anything like what they found. We certainly must have looked like an unlikely crew."

"I wonder how many other surprises are lurking under parking lots in the city?" James said.

"I'm not going looking," I responded tartly. "Let Marty deal with that—it's more her style. Does it strike you as strange that a body sat there under a crumbling building for, oh, a century or two? Or maybe not—you remember how many abandoned buildings we discovered there are in the city, not long ago, and nobody's going to invest time and money in tearing them down—unless it's someone running for mayor who wants to improve the appearance of our fair city. Actually, they'd be more likely to pretty up Independence Mall than North Philadelphia. At the same time, there's been a lot of construction in that area even in the few years I've been working in the city. There's I-95, which must have been a big mess to build. Come to think of it, I read that they didn't bother with any official archeologists—the road builders just started building and buried whatever they found. It's understandable, I guess, since they were in a hurry, but imagine what artifacts they must have covered over. Same thing with Independence Mall. Again, I understand why the city wanted a good setting for Independence Hall, but what's under the grass there? Funny how attitudes toward history change over time. Some people were really upset when they excavated what was Washington's house near there and found it had slave quarters."

"Have you found any interesting relics around our house?"

"A couple of broken bottles. A lot of rusty cut nails. I haven't done much gardening, so there may be more. But I don't have time to look. So, what do you think will happen next?"

James said firmly, "Marty will figure out the proper city authorities to contact and lean on them to get something done about it. And fill Barney in, I assume. No doubt she will draft you to help, and any other members of the historical community who are interested. As for the body, I don't know. Do you think it's possible that it's an ancestor of hers? You said at least one lived right around there, back in seventeen-whatever."

"Since it's Marty, it's always possible. Should somebody keep a guard on the site? Would the police do that, or would Barney have to hire someone? I can just see strollers passing by on the street thinking a skull just lying there on the ground would look great on their man-cave mantelpiece."

"Nell, you have a strange imagination. Anything else you want to worry about?"

"Food."

"Take-out again?" James quirked an eyebrow at me.

"How about someone who delivers? I'm not sure they'd let us in the door, looking the way we do now."

"Good point. Home, then phone for food."

When we arrived, I let James manage the food while I went up to take a fast shower. When I came down, toweling my hair dry, he'd already poured two glasses of wine. Anything stronger and I thought I'd fall asleep with my face in my dinner.

We settled in comfortable chairs to wait for the delivery. "Don't you just love these unexpected events?" I asked James.

"I hope you're being sarcastic. But at least nobody's been shooting at us."

"They've all been dead for at least a century, so that's unlikely. Is there any crime involved?"

"I doubt it. Somebody messed up with the cemetery. I can't imagine anyone associated with a church would simply bury the buried, so to speak, simply to build a new building on the site. The parishioners would have pitched a fit!"

"You'd think so, wouldn't you? But how on earth would you go about covering up so much space, filled with not just bodies but a fair number of coffins and maybe some headstones, without anybody noticing what you were doing? Even if you did it at night, that's a lot of ground to cover. Oops, sorry, bad pun."

"Burying dozens of the dead at one time is not my area of expertise. Nor was I ever in the military, so I did not observe the process. But I'm sure between all of us we can find an expert."

"Let's hope so!" I said firmly. "This is definitely not in my job description."

The food arrived, we ate, and as I had predicted, my eyes would not stay open. After a huge yawn I asked James, "Marty and I thought we should meet at the Society tomorrow and do some research. Better her than me—she can get that done quickly. I'm surprised that she never looked up that house, but maybe she really was terrified at what she'd seen and tried to blot it out."

"You and Marty can start with finding out when that house was built, and then abandoned. And who the cemetery belonged to and when it was shut down. They must have coincided at some point."

"Maybe that's why General Terwilliger moved away from the river—he'd had enough of staring at graves."

"I don't suppose there would be a record at the Society of who spread asphalt or whatever was used before? The graves must have been hard to miss."

"We don't keep many commercial or industrial records at the Society, unless they intersect with important people. Church records, maybe. But you're right—that would have been a big job. We can look at maps, I suppose—it should be possible to determine when that cemetery disappeared from a dated map. Not that anyone would have labeled a parking lot. Maybe there's something in documents relating to the I-95 construction, although I wouldn't know where they'd be stored. Or even if they survived. But I will look. Can I go to bed now? Marty's an early riser, and she'd probably like to see me at dawn. Thank goodness she has a key to the Society."

. . .

The phone range at dawn. James, accustomed to phone calls that usually signaled some sort of crisis, was out of bed and down the hall and talking before I managed to get my eyes open. I couldn't hear what he was saying, but I didn't have a good feeling about it. I wished I could just put a pillow over my head and go back to sleep.

That was not to be. He was back inside of two minutes and sat on the edge of the bed. "That was Martha."

"Why am I not surprised?" I pulled myself up into a sitting position. "What's going on?"

"She couldn't find Barney yesterday."

"She calls us at dawn to tell us that?" I demanded.

"She's worried. What with this bunch of bodies showing up, she thought he'd be all over it. And he left before we found the other body, so he doesn't know about all that."

"That's true, although it may not have anything to do with his plans. I can't say how well Marty knows Barney—she knows a *lot* of people. Maybe he went off to some bar to drown his sorrows over the mess his construction project has become."

"Do you know anything more about Barney?" James asked.

"No. I don't even know how much Marty knows. She said she'd been at school with his sister, but I forget where she went to school. Someplace that probably cost a lot of money, with plenty of alumni whose names you would recognize from the news. Sorry, that sounds kind of snide, but you know what I mean."

"I do. Among other things, it probably means that Barney didn't have any sort of criminal record. That's all?"

"Yup," I told James. "It takes quite a while to get to know as many people as she does. So, we assume Marty was working her network last night, trying to track Barney down, but she failed to find him. She seems to be worried about that. Now she wants us to worry too. Great way to start the day," I grumbled.

"When was he last seen?" James asked, not unreasonably.

"Dylan was hunting for skeletons with him, and then he left to get us all some water. When Dylan came back, Barney was gone. He didn't say anything to Dylan about leaving, but he never reappeared."

"Nell, don't get too bent out of shape. This doesn't have to mean anything. Maybe he just fell into a grave and bashed his head."

I glared at him. "James, you're not making me feel any better about this. Isn't two hundred-plus bodies in a day enough? Did Marty say we should go meet her?"

"For all you know there are more than two hundred bodies, and yes—she'll be waiting for us at the site. Remember, as far as we know Marty was the only person who knew about the hole under that building, and the four of us are the only people who know what's in it. Barney wasn't there."

"Maybe. Or maybe he did. Barney did have a work team there, and any of them could have been poking around."

"And no doubt they'd have made a big thing of it. Let's stick with the basic assumption that we four—plus Marty's cousins, whoever they were—are the only ones who know what we found. Unless Barney found it on his own. We don't know who that man was."

I rolled over and stared at the ceiling. "Okay, let's take a step back. Barney and his crew discovered a whole lot of bodies. Who were they supposed to tell? There were too many to just pour concrete over them and start building, and I'd imagine that his construction crew might object to that."

"The police," James said flatly. "They're unidentified bodies and we don't know how they died. Ergo, they must be investigated."

"Can we hope that our favorite detective will be in charge of the case?"

"Detective Hrivnak? Quite possibly. After all, it's practically in her backyard."

"Good. At least she's smart, and I think we mended a few fences the last time we worked together. But we're going to have a lot to explain if we throw in the other body."

"She should be used to that, after working with us before. So you'd better get up and get dressed. I'll make coffee, and then we'll go meet Marty. And if the police aren't already involved, it would fall to me to contact them."

"Are we going to the Society, to Marty's house, or to police headquarters? Or to the work site?"

James stood up. "Nell, I have had one three-minute conversation with Martha Terwilliger this morning, and she said she'd be at the construction site. I think we should cut to the chase and go straight to headquarters, once we collect Marty."

"And how much do we tell them? As in, do we include the body in the hole?"

"We can talk about it on the way in to the city. But my first response is to tell them everything we know. Which is not much. But we don't want to look like we have anything to hide. Because we don't."

"Then it shouldn't take long."

Chapter Ten

So much for the nice, peaceful weekend I had fantasized about, the one where I planted geraniums or petunias or whatever else might grow in Chestnut Hill, and James put on an old T-shirt and mowed the lawn. Instead we were driving back to the city to meet with the Philadelphia police. What fun.

I called Marty on my cell phone, and she answered quickly. "Where are you?" I asked before she could speak.

"Still at my house. After I talked to James I figured it would take you a little time to reach the city."

"Anything from Barney yet?"

"No. Where are you going?"

"Police HQ. James thought we should come clean. And that means about everything. What we know about the lost cemetery, and the body we found. I'm hoping we'll find Detective Hrivnak there."

"I'll meet you there, then. You want to give up the body under the house?" Marty sounded incredulous.

"I think we should, and James agrees. It's not like we know anything about him, except that you can tell her how long you knew he'd been there. And we're not responsible for him in any way. I'm hoping that we can persuade the police to treat him gently until we figure out what's going on. But I can't believe she's going to want to pack up all those other bodies—they can't possibly be evidence of anything now, and Barney couldn't possibly have hidden their existence for long. Could be some descendent went berserk when he found out that six-times-great-grandfather Aloysius had been lying in the mud since 1820. But if we get in front of this, maybe she'll let us help. Given the age of the bodies, we could be the best people to ask."

Marty gave a distinctly unladylike snort. "But I do have some concerns about the body under the house."

"You know any important people in the historical archeology

community in the city who will answer your phone call at this ungodly hour?"

"Probably. I'll get to work on it."

"Great. We should call Dylan. But I don't have his number with me."

"I haven't heard from him. Do we need him?"

"Not really. I just want to be sure we have all our stories straight. So, James and I will meet you at HQ in about half an hour, and we will tell them everything we know."

"Yes. You're right, Nell—you and I are better equipped to figure out who the bodies are—all of them—and how they all came to be there than the police force is. And they should trust us by now."

"I agree. See you soon." I hung up.

"Any news?" James asked, his eyes on the road.

"Ha, ha. I know Marty seems to feel some proprietary interest in the body—and I suppose in the neighborhood as well, since she has family ties there—but we haven't done anything wrong, unless you count not reporting the body that we found the minute we discovered it. We were there yesterday because we happened to find an old map and we were curious. We didn't exactly expect Barney to find a couple hundred skeletons, nor were we looking for a secret hidden under an abandoned building. But if the police department wants answers, we're the best people to talk to. Except for legally, I guess. Somebody's going to have to move all those bodies to a final resting place."

"What do you think happened to Barney?" James asked. "Why isn't he at the site?"

"I have no idea. I just met him. I've probably seen his name, or his company name, on signs at construction sites, but apart from that I can't tell you if he's honest or crooked, smart or stupid. Marty didn't mention any problems with him, personal or professional. So he found a bunch of bones in the lot he was planning to build on. There are simply too many to hide, so one could argue that he called in the professionals—that'd be Marty and me. He figured Marty could help him, and he was hoping to make the best of things and to avoid jamming up his project. It's not clear whether he knew about the other body, and it wasn't on any part of his property, as far as I know. Of course, Barney may have wondered why Marty was wandering around over there—if he was even still around to notice. I'd love to know where he went, since he was the one who invited us. But I have no reason *not* to trust him, if that makes sense."

"Tread lightly, Nell. The police are going to be in charge of this investigation—Hrivnak and her crew, most likely. If you're lucky and make nice to her, she might share details."

"Let's hope so."

I hesitated before asking my next question. "I don't want to be an alarmist, but do you think anybody who mattered saw us wandering around where we found the last body and thought we knew something? I mean, could anyone else know about it, apart from Marty's cousins? Maybe Barney stumbled on it while he was just sniffing around, but didn't want to share his information?"

"Seems unlikely, doesn't it?" James said reasonably. "He's a building contractor—he builds buildings. He's not an archeologist. Most likely his first priority at the moment is getting all those cemetery bodies removed so he can start construction."

"I know that. But coincidences are starting to pile up. What're the odds that Dylan would find a scrap of paper in a book nobody had looked at in years, and it would lead us right to that particular building? Next to a whole lot of other bodies? And Barney just happens to call Marty the same day and ask for her help to deal with what used to be a cemetery?"

"Nell, are you looking for something to worry about? Don't go overboard until you have all available information. Maybe Barney is exactly who he appears to be, and he already knew Marty and she was the first friend he thought of to call. End of story."

We'd reached the city, and I told him Marty was going to meet us at police headquarters. James found a parking space near the Roundhouse, Philadelphia's distinctive police headquarters, and we walked to the front entrance, where we found Marty waiting. There was no sign of Dylan, so Marty hadn't been able to reach him, and I wondered if Detective Hrivnak even knew of his existence. It wasn't as though we'd all signed a register to look at the field of bones.

"Hi, Marty," I said. "Any word from Dylan?"

"No," she said tersely. "I don't have his phone number, and he doesn't have mine. Anyway, we can describe how we found the map—which will also explain why James was there—and why Barney called me."

"It shouldn't seem mysterious, Marty. We were doing our jobs, or at least I was. I suppose I'm the one who started the whole thing. I could have told Dylan to ignore that pitiful piece of paper he'd found and get back to work, and that would have been the end of it. Or I could have let him show me and seen that the note was unreadable and filed it away for some future research, rather than asking James's people to take a look at it. But I decided to call you, and you know what happened after that. None of us thought anything we were doing was important—we were just curious about why it had survived and what it might mean."

"I know, I know. But then it got more complicated. And personal."

"Marty," James said, "did Barney see the map?"

"No. I might have mentioned it, but he was much more interested in the bones, and in getting his project started—he's got money invested in it. He thought I might be able to speed things up."

"Did he say whether anyone has an issue with the building project?" James asked. "I mean, before the bones were found."

"Not that I know of," Marty told him. "It's not too large, and it's in a desirable part of town, and Barney told me he filled out all the right forms. I've seen some of the plans and drawings for the project and it looks like it fits the neighborhood. And as far as we know, nobody else—living, anyway, except my cousins—knew about the

71

other body, so they couldn't complain about it. Maybe they will now, when the news gets out. Nobody's going to be able to keep this quiet."

"And here we are, talking to the police once again." I sighed. "Another item that wasn't in my job description."

Like good schoolchildren the three of us marched into the vestibule, and James explained to the officer on duty what we were doing there. Somebody called upstairs, and we waited until we saw Detective Hrivnak emerge from the elevator. I tried to remember the last time we had seen her but couldn't. All I knew was that it was too often, although she was competent and good at her job. I hoped we'd be in and out quickly.

"Well, well," she said when she greeted us. "Nell, James and Ms. Terwilliger, together again. I thought things were a little too quiet. You're here about that cemetery that got itself discovered?" When we all nodded, she added, "Come on upstairs and we can talk."

We all were silent in the elevator, and when the doors opened she led us to a small conference room and shut the door. We found seats around a table and stared at her.

I decided to get things moving. "So you know why we're here?"

She nodded. "I figured you had to be involved somehow. Besides, you ran into two street cops when you were there yesterday, right? Agent Morrison here flashed his FBI credentials, and the cops remembered. I figured the two women had to be you and probably Ms. Terwilliger here. You happen to know where Barney Taylor is? The police need to talk with him, since he's in charge of that project."

"No, Detective," I said. "He was around for a while, after we arrived, but he left the place before we did."

"He didn't happen to mention where he was going? He's not at home or at his office."

"Nope. We were kind of busy counting corpses, and he didn't say goodbye. Have you looked at the site?"

"You've really outdone yourselves this time. You didn't find just one body, you found a couple of hundred all in one place. Yes, I took a look early this morning. Creepy. Care to explain what you were doing there?"

Marty and I exchanged glances, and I launched into the explanation of my intern Dylan finding the piece of paper and extricating it from the binding, and then the two of us taking it to the FBI lab, and then showing it to Marty, and then our plan to go look at the site, after Marty had talked with Barney. "So we spent most of yesterday afternoon trying to assess just how many bodies there were in this plot of ground that nobody seemed to know about. Barney disappeared at some point midafternoon, but none of us noticed he was gone, and he didn't tell anyone he was leaving. But he seemed to be grateful that we were there and checking things out, because between us Marty and I have a good chance of determining why there were bodies there at all, much less so many. We have a lot of records at the Society, and we know people we can talk to in the city. But Barney did say he'd checked the official records when he filed for a building permit, and nothing out of the ordinary turned up."

I relaxed just a bit. "Okay, your turn, Detective. What happened?"

She leaned back, stared at the ceiling, and started reciting. "I understand that Barney called Ms. Terwilliger here first, and you went to the site with Barney yesterday to check it out. The police were not aware of the discovery of human remains at the site until Saturday, when they found you at the site. Our department was kind of busy—tourist season, you know—so we couldn't send anyone to check it out right away. All this was after you found this map you were talking about? Then Barney left midafternoon and you didn't see him after that. Is that correct?"

Marty, James and I looked at each other, and I responded, "Yes. We left the site about four, and he hadn't returned by then."

"I tried calling him after I got home," Marty volunteered, "but he didn't answer. He hadn't left a message on my phones either."

The detective nodded. "We have regular patrols for that area, especially in the summer, because it's so busy, but no one saw or heard anything unusual, so maybe he didn't come back later."

"Was there anything missing? Machinery or equipment?" James asked.

"Was it a robbery, you mean? Not that we could tell. Work hadn't really started, except for removing the parking lot paving, so mostly there were shovels and wheelbarrows. Nothing valuable." Hrivnak slumped in her chair. "This investigation is going to be a bitch, er, bear. I almost hate to admit it, but since you and Ms. Terwilliger know so much about old Philadelphia, I figure you can help. James here is just a bonus."

"Thanks . . . I think," I told her, and then I glanced at Marty, who gave a small nod. "But there's one more piece of the puzzle that we ought to tell you about, although it may not have anything to do with the construction site."

"There's more? Okay, I'm listening."

Marty finally spoke up. "There's another body that you may not have found yet, but it's close. And it's an old body—I mean, *really* old. But it could be important, and we need to tell you about it."

Chapter Eleven

"So spill it. I've got a couple of hundred bodies to investigate," Detective Hrivnak said impatiently.

Marty took a deep breath and started. "When I was a kid, my cousins and I used to hang out in that neighborhood and explore. One day we were snooping around one of the falling-down buildings on the east side of Arch Street. There was a hole in the foundation big enough for a skinny kid to crawl through, so of course we did. And we found a body."

Detective Hrivnak didn't seem surprised, but then, she knew Marty. "And who did you tell about this?"

"Nobody. Maybe we weren't sure it was real or that we'd really seen it, but it scared us. And it was an old body—still had what was left of its clothes on. Or at least it did nearly half a century ago. My cousins and I agreed not to talk about it, and to the best of my knowledge no one ever did. That was one of the reasons I wanted to go back and see the place now, to see if maybe I'd just imagined it."

"So now I'm supposed to add another body to the list of unknown victims?" The detective did not seem pleased.

"That's not all," Marty said reluctantly "First, let me say that I didn't tell Barney about it yesterday. I figured the place where I'd seen that body wasn't on his lot anyway, so he didn't need to know. Second, it was too far away to have been part of the cemetery, if that's what it was. It was under a house, and the house was old."

"Go on," Hrivnak said.

"So Nell and Dylan and James and I went looking for the house. I was pretty sure it was still standing, though nobody's lived there for a long time—one of those unclaimed buildings in the city that nobody knew what to do with. I had sort of been keeping an eye on it when I happened to be down there, but I never went near it again. Well, we found the house, and we found the hole in the house that we'd climbed into all those years ago. Of course, now we're a bit older and definitely larger, but Dylan volunteered to see if he'd fit through the hole, and he'd brought a camera with him."

"Detective," James added, "that's not as stupid as it sounds. I was there, and I kept hold of Dylan's legs, so if it looked like things were going south I could haul him out quickly. Luckily I didn't have to."

Hrivnak glared at him briefly before going on. "And? Should I guess that he found something?"

"Yes, he did," Marty said. "When Dylan crawled out he showed us the pictures he'd taken. Remember, we were looking at small screenshots only, but they showed that he found a body. *The* body, the one I remembered."

"Hold on," Hrivnak said. "You're saying there really was a body in that hole? The same one you remembered?"

"Yes. The cousins and I had been so panicked that we got out of there fast. And we hadn't brought flashlights or anything like that. We'd never planned to go exploring—our parents would have pitched a fit if they had known."

"Not a new body?"

"From Dylan's pictures we didn't think so. They were only snapshots. But the body definitely was not modern. Not some poor homeless guy who wandered in there and never came out, or a tourist who got mugged and was stuffed away out of sight."

"And you didn't see any reason to mention this?"

"Well, no—we were still debating about what to do. Barney didn't seem to know anything about it—at least, he didn't say anything about it—and I had my own reasons for wanting to know more. I figured once the body was officially found, we'd lose any chance to learn anything from it. I'd like to think it's historical, but we haven't had time to check. We need better pictures. Dylan's pictures were good enough to identify what's in there as a body, but that's about all."

Hrivnak shut her eyes for a moment, then looked at us again. "Let me get this straight. Barney wants to build apartments on that main lot, but when he started digging he finds a couple of hundred skeletons. He stops digging and talks to you because he knows you know a lot about local history plus you've got connections with the city. You and your pals here come trotting over to see what's what. Ms. Terwilliger, you don't bother to mention the other body stuffed under a nearby house, but you invite your friends here to check it out, to see if you really saw what you thought you saw. You never mentioned it to Barney, and he left before you found it. Have I got it right so far?"

We all nodded like marionettes.

Hrivnak continued, "So then you got Dylan to sneak under the house and take some pictures and they confirmed it was a body. And you still didn't tell anyone."

"That was only yesterday!" Marty protested. "Nell, help me out here."

"Detective," I began in what I hoped was a soothing voice, "I'm not criticizing the police department, but we were afraid that if we told your department, you'd sweep in and clear everything out, and we'd lose anything like a historical context. Even in the best case, you probably would have lumped the outlier in with all the other bodies," I ended dubiously.

"I'd like to see the ME handle a couple of hundred bodies at once—he'd probably have to rent New Jersey to store them," Hrivnak muttered. Then she straightened up and said firmly, "There are police protocols to follow when a body is found."

"Of course there are," I said, nodding, "but what if that body is two hundred years old? Do you treat it the same way you would treat a fresh body?"

"I can't say I've ever had that problem," she admitted. "Most of our victims are a bit newer."

"So let me ask you this: can we help? Or rather, will you let us help? I mean, not with analyzing corpses, but with finding out who they are and how they all came to be where they are. That would mean we'd like to have you leave them *in situ* for a bit so we could get the right kind of analysis done, with the right kind of people, but that might be only a couple of days. We could work with the medical examiner, if that's what it takes."

"I'm going to have to think about it," the detective said. "And how the hell do we handle the press? I mean, it's kind of hard to hide a block full of skeletons in plain view. It's gotta be, what, a few acres?"

"Three or four, I'd guess," I told her.

Hrivnak went on, "The lot has a fence around it, but anyone could see right through it. You could cover it with something, but there are taller buildings around it, so plenty of people would be able to see all those bodies. Skeletons."

"I think that rather than try to hide the whole thing, you—we—could get ahead of the story. Find a friendly reporter and involve him—or her—from the beginning," I suggested. "Emphasize the history, not the creepy parts. I'd be happy to help with that."

"I bet you would." The detective thought for a moment. "Look, this mess is going to take clearances from half the city departments. Don't ask me to decide right now, but maybe I can give you an answer about your idea tomorrow."

"That's fine—I know what problems you must be facing."

"If I may make a suggestion," James interrupted, "I think you need to provide some sort of protection for the site, once its location becomes known. I know that will involve extra expense for your department, but otherwise you may lose valuable evidence. The chain-link fence that's there now is not going to be enough to keep people out."

"Maybe we can find a donor from the local historic community, if we emphasize the need to protect this unique part of the city's past," I suggested. I had no idea if it was possible, but it was worth looking into. Marty was sure to know someone who'd be interested—and she already had a stake in the investigation.

"Whatever," Hrivnak said. "Let me touch base with my boss and whatever other departments are going to have to be involved. I see your point, but I'll have to convince the rest of 'em. I'll get back to you when I know something."

"Thank you!" I said, and I meant it. This was a unique if weird opportunity to learn something new about the city, and I wanted to be kept in the loop.

"And find that guy Dylan, will you? He's got to be a witness of something, and he's got the camera, right? Even if he doesn't know anything, I've got to check him off the interview list."

"I've got his contact information back at the Society," I said. "I'll look it up and let you know where he should be."

Detective Hrivnak stood up quickly. "I'll walk you out." We followed like a flock of sheep, and she let us out the door.

When we reached the outside world, it was still the same day. The sun was shining, and a few cars honked at one another. I took a deep breath. "Why did I expect to get arrested? We're on good terms with Hrivnak, aren't we?"

"I think we've done our share of favors for her, so we're about even," James said.

"You were quiet in there," I said.

"You two are the historians. I'm the bodyguard. Or something like that."

"Marty? You all right?"

"What?" She looked like she was coming out of a trance. "Oh. I'm running through my mental Rolodex to figure out who I should call. As an optimist I'll assume the detective can pull a few official strings and let us have access to the site, but as a pessimist I'm sure the allotted time will be short, and we've got a lot to do. Where do you think Dylan is? He seemed really gung-ho yesterday."

"Our original plan was to meet at the Society today," I reminded her. "He may be working there, and you said you couldn't reach him by phone to tell him otherwise."

"Maybe. Can we sit for a couple of minutes and just breathe, and think?" Marty said plaintively. "It's too nice a day to sit inside the Society building."

"Okay. Independence Mall?" I suggested.

"If it's not too crowded and we don't have to duck Frisbees."

"Works for me." I turned to James. "Is there anything you need or want to do today?"

He smiled. "What, and miss the chance to identify a couple of hundred bodies all at once? There might be some sort of FBI prize for that, as long as there's no war or famine or plague attached."

"Then let's sit down and map out a strategy." To demonstrate, I found an empty bench on one edge of the Mall and sat. Marty and James joined me, more slowly.

I took the lead. "Okay, assume we have limited time. What do we need to know, and where do we find it?"

"A history of early Philadelphia cemeteries," Marty said quickly. "I can't imagine that a city block's worth of bodies would have been forgotten entirely. There must be a record somewhere."

"All right. James, what legalities do we need to know?"

"I don't know what you mean," he said.

"Who's legally responsible for the former cemetery and its occupants? Is there a court procedure to follow? Please don't tell me someone has to identify each and every one, even if it's possible with DNA these days. And if they've been dead for a hundred years or more, on average, there are probably no descendants to match. So we're back to the first point: find out what cemeteries are missing, so to speak, and see if somewhere in the city there's a list of burials for them." I hesitated a moment. "You know, I feel very crass, but I keep thinking of the PR value of this, if we handle it right. Of course the press is going to be involved, at least while the story is still fresh. There must be some local scholars who'd like to get an oar in. The Society could set up an exhibit of what was found and what was done with it, and offer workshops on how to identify old bodies. And so on."

"I like it," Marty said firmly, "but first we have to identify the bodies. Was there a church that went with the cemetery?"

"You tell me. It was your ancestors who lived in that neighborhood. Did they leave any diaries or anything? Or do you know what church they belonged to locally? It could be that the local cemetery wasn't exactly intended for the wealthy upper class. And why did your ancestors move uptown? Were they uncomfortable living next to the dead?"

"You don't ask much, do you, Nell?"

"Look, I'm just spitballing here. These are things we *could* do. The question is, which ones have to be done first, while the others wait for more time and possibly funding?"

"Fair enough," Marty agreed.

"And one more question," I went on. "While we're putting together our wish list—Marty, do you want to focus on the single body? It could be related to the cemetery, or it could be something else entirely."

"I probably do have some insider information about that neighborhood at the right time," she said. "That single body is under police jurisdiction in this case, as much as all the others, but I think we can finagle control over that."

"We still haven't figured out where Barney is," James said suddenly.

Marty glanced at her phone. "He hasn't called me," Marty said. "He should be all over this. It's his project, and for him, the longer the delays, the more money he loses."

"Marty, how well do you know Barney?"

"Not very," she said. "Socially only, I guess. Too bad Dylan isn't here—he could do some background research on Barney. It wouldn't take him long."

"So we need to find both Dylan and Barney. Let's get something to eat, then go over to the Society and figure out what resources we have to work with," I said.

"I for one would like to look at maps of the neighborhood," Marty said. "Ones big enough to see details."

"Good idea. I can look into early church history, and then we can compare notes—there should be some overlap. And you're going to want to look at who owned the houses along the street there. Why would there be a body there?"

"Definitely."

Chapter Twelve

We had good intentions. We even had a plan, more or less. But I was ready for a nap. It had been a very odd few days, with a resulting body count of a couple hundred or so. I didn't know anything about those, or what was left of them, but given my professional position, I thought I should, so I felt guilty. At least Marty hadn't known any more than I did about the lost cemetery. But she had known about the other body—and now maybe she was feeling guilty about not telling anyone for half a century. What would I have done? I had no idea. Still, only our little group and a few of her many cousins knew what she knew.

"Is it still Sunday?" I asked.

"Last time I checked," James told me. "What do you want to do next?"

"I wish I knew. Did we eat lunch?"

"No, but that can be fixed. But then what?"

"Well, as you may recall, since it's Sunday there's no one at the Society because we're not open. There won't be anyone there tomorrow either—we're closed on Monday too. So we should take advantage of the peace and quiet—and lack of competition for resources. We can get in a few hours today and at least figure out what we need to look at. I'm going to check on church histories, and will look at who lived in that neighborhood and whose house she were crawling under. Could be that body was the owner, or it could be someone else, from some other period. Or whatever the earlier equivalent of a street person was—a stranger who had no particular reason to be there. Checking that out will give Dylan something to do if we find him. James, anything you want to do? You're kind of the odd man out here."

"I am at your service," James said, deliberately pompously. "Just remember, this is my day off."

"How about this? We go to the Society and hope that Dylan is there and didn't think to contact us. Before all this started I asked him to pull together the rest of the Featherstone book collection and see if there are any other mysterious pieces of paper attached to anything. Don't worry, Marty—I told him not to tear anything apart, but if there are other bindings as poorly attached as that first one, he shouldn't have any problem figuring out where to look."

James stood up from the bench and almost shook himself like a dog. "I vote that I go get food for all of us, while you two go to the Society and dig in. Where do you want to work?"

"Someplace where we won't be bothered. But it might be a good idea to start with the maps, so we'd need to find a place to spread things out, at least in the beginning. Does that work for you, Marty?"

"I guess. It's so odd, thinking about researching a part of the city I would have said I knew well, but when I was there on the construction site yesterday, it seemed unfamiliar. That's the problem with history—we say things are old, but we forget that they keep changing, even while we watch."

"Well, try to look at it all with fresh eyes, as though you'd never seen it before. Maybe that will help."

I stood up, hoping that would get my blood flowing again. "Okay, let's go. James—food. Marty, the Society. Meet us there, James."

"Yes, ma'am," he said with a mock-military tone. "I'll call your cell when I arrive."

We parted ways, Marty and I heading for the Society building, James toward Market Street, where there would bound to be many food choices, even on a Sunday.

For a block or two Marty was silent. Finally she said, "Doesn't this all seem weird to you?"

"What, finding a couple of hundred bodies? Plus one?"

"Well, yes. But first Dylan found that map, and showed it to me, and I recognized it, and we made a beeline for the place, and presto, there was a body I hadn't thought of for more than half my life."

"Synchronicity?" I asked.

"I'll settle for coincidence. Unless of course Dylan finds a manuscript that explains everything."

"That would be helpful," I said.

It didn't take us long to reach the Society, and I always carried my keys with me for occasions like this. I unlocked the door, then let Marty enter. Inside I inhaled deeply: the place was silent and no lights were on, but I loved the smell of old paper and leather. "Map room?" I asked Marty.

"Yes. Drat, I keep forgetting to carry a camera, and my cell phone isn't good enough to take detailed pictures. You should buy a couple of cameras for this place."

"Of course," I said. "I should always be prepared to find more bodies and need to do immediate research on them. Let's go up." I checked to make sure my phone was on, since James was going to call, then led the way to the large workroom on the second floor. I turned on the lights, and then I realized there was someone in the room: Dylan.

"Hey," he greeted Marty and me. "Where've you been?"

"At police headquarters. James and I decided it was the right thing to do, to explain what we knew to the police. I would have called you about the change of plans, but I didn't have your phone number handy. And how'd you get in?"

"I got a key when I got the internship—don't worry, it's official, and I signed some document," Dylan said. "I figured you'd show up here eventually. Why did you need to talk to the police?"

"In case you don't know—and I don't know why you would—the police and/or the medical examiner are required to attend to any body, even if it's been dead for a couple of centuries," I told him. "Anyway, Detective Hrivnak was kind of expecting us because apparently the officers from yesterday reported that they'd seen several rather odd people nosing around the site. That would be us. But she and I have worked together before and she trusts us. She said we could help with the historical aspects, and I practically kissed her. I can't bear the thought that a gang of guys with wheelbarrows might show up and cart all the corpses away and file them somewhere."

"And did you tell her about Marty's body?"

"Yes—it seemed smart to come clean all at once. And if we want to have a prayer of identifying that one, we need to preserve as much evidence as possible."

"Good point. Well, I came in to see if I could enlarge the pictures of Marty's dead guy, and then I wanted to finish gathering up the Featherstone books, like you asked."

"Have you found anything?"

"No, not yet. First I had to find them and sort them—they were kind of scattered in different places in the building, wherever there was room—and I haven't gotten around to examining them. Are we making a big leap of logic to think that the map we found means anything? It was just kind of stuffed into the binding of that book, and it's not like anybody would find it unless they knew exactly what book it was in. And an amateur wouldn't be able to get it out of the book without making a mess."

"That's a good point, Dylan, but I thought we should check anyway. I should go pull Harriet Featherstone's file and see if anybody left any personal comments about her in it. I don't know her genealogy, and I can't recall if she ever talked about it. But as Marty pointed out, there may be some cosmic meaning to the fact that we found the letter and the body within a day of each other. It's worth looking into."

"Are you going to stay here now?"

"James is bringing food. I was going to check out Philadelphia church history to see if we can figure out if the cemetery was connected to a church, and Marty was going to look at early city maps and see if she could find out whose house that was. That should be enough for today, and we've both got tomorrow free."

"I'm really enjoying this, you know," Dylan said shyly. "Maybe I should look at the Featherstone file first? Maybe there's something personal about her that would explain what that paper was doing in a book at all. Or the paper might not even have been hers, just something a random bookbinder picked up and recycled."

"It's possible. How many books did she leave us?"

"I think around two thousand, but that's just a guess. You told me she was ninety-something, right? She'd been collecting for a long time."

"In case you haven't figured it out yet, collecting is a passion. Or an obsession. Once you're hooked, you can't stop yourself."

Dylan grinned. "I get it. Do I get to eat with you guys?"

"Sure. I'll come find you when James gets here, and we can eat in the break room."

We split up then. I went back to my office and turned on my computer so I could search for references on churches of Philadelphia during its first centuries, and the cemeteries that might have belonged to them. I admit to a surprising fondness for old cemeteries —I usually stopped at the Christ Church Cemetery to visit with Ben Franklin and others, and I knew Marty had some ancestors buried there. No, the dead don't talk to me, although I've been known to talk to them, but doing this makes me feel closer to them. And I'm not alone: you can tell where the famous people were buried in a cemetery by where the biggest crowd is standing. Which again made me wonder, how do you simply cover over a fairly substantial-sized cemetery and forget about it? Yet that's what we thought had happened.

I had jotted down a number of references when my cell phone rang. It was James and he was waiting downstairs, so I went down to let him in.

"Hey there," I greeted him. "We found Dylan—he was hard at work trying to pull together all the Featherstone books in one place. I told him you were bringing food. Let's eat in the break room—I live in terror of getting greasy fingerprints and crumbs on any parts of the collections."

"Sounds good," he said.

I turned and led him up the grand staircase to the second floor. "Detective Hrivnak was going to check with the authorities in the city about what to do with the bodies?" James asked on the way up. "And what the timeline will be?"

"That's what she said. I'm sure she doesn't want that big patch of bodies in her backyard, so to speak, and they can't just leave them there the way they are."

"She didn't seem exactly fascinated by the history of the place."

"No, she's a very pragmatic person—but she does get the job done. I'm glad she's willing to keep us in the loop."

"She's a useful friend to have, given your track record."

"Too true."

James and I joined Dylan and Marty in the break room at the back of the building and ate quickly. "Dylan, do you know where the donor and member files are kept?" I asked. "If not, I can show you and give you the Featherstone file so you can look through it. Although I warn you—most of the comments are about financial status and potential donations."

"Thanks, Nell," he said. "I don't expect any amazing discoveries, but at least I'll have a sense of the person behind the collection."

"My mother used to play bridge with her, years back," Marty volunteered. "Which doesn't tell you much about her personally, except that she could keep track of cards. And she stayed active until the end."

"You never know what will turn out to be important," I said in a mock-serious tone. "Are we finished eating? Because I don't think I'll last more than another couple of hours, and I'd like to get at least something done."

"I'm ready," Marty declared. "I'm going to pull the relevant maps and see if I can match them up with the 1790 census. Yeah, I know, people moved around a lot back then, especially early on when the city was growing fast, and I wouldn't swear to how complete or accurate the censuses are, but it's a place to start."

"Happy hunting!" I told her. "James, do you have something to keep you busy, or would you rather go home? I can take the train back."

"I've always got paperwork at the office. Give me a call when you're ready to leave." With a backward wave, he left.

I went back to my office to make more lists of source materials. When I had collected a handful of call numbers for books and manuscripts in the Society's collections, I went wandering in the stacks to hunt them down. Two hours later I was definitely getting bleary-eyed, until I looked at the last couple of sources I had pulled off the shelf and realized that I held the answer in my hand. Or rather, two answers. Number one: the missing church had been the First Baptist Church, founded in 1698. The congregation had moved around for a while until they took over a meetinghouse at Second and Market street—which would have been half a block north of where the orphaned cemetery was found. That church had been rebuilt more than once, then relocated to a different location in 1900, and it finally merged with another church.

So, bottom line: the church that the original cemetery had belonged to was long gone physically. What had happened to the cemetery?

And then I realized I also had that answer in front of me, in the form of a small newspaper announcement dating to 1860, which declared that the church had made "arrangements for the removal of the dead from their old burial ground, Second Street, below Arch, to their new ground (Mount Moriah Cemetery)." It seemed from the clipping that the church committee was still hanging out at the original site in case anyone wanted to remove their loved ones or buy a new lot in the other cemetery.

But the transfer had never happened, or only some of it had. It appeared that many of the burials had indeed been moved to Mount Moriah, where they occupied their own section. I had to wonder what the original total of the burials had been, if "most" were moved but a couple hundred had been left behind. I also wondered if the church records had moved along with the church at one time or another, or if they had found their way to one or another library, or if they'd been lost altogether. Of course, there was always the chance that once a major part of the transfer had taken place, the church ran out of money and energy and conveniently lost the paperwork on the rest, meanwhile shoveling dirt over the remaining burials. That had remained the church's dirty little secret—yes, a bad pun. Was it legal? I was getting spacey, and it was time to call it a day. There was no doubt more research to be done, but it could wait for one more day.

Chapter Thirteen

Even though I was pretty much seeing cross-eyed, I felt proud. I'd actually solved one part of the mystery: to which church did the old cemetery belong? Of course, that had revealed another mystery: why had only part of the cemetery been moved to its new location? Had the church forgotten about hundreds of bodies? Run out of time and money? But how could they have callously just paved over them? But the church itself had changed locations and been rebuilt more than once. Still, it was troubling. I wasn't sure whether I hoped the solution turned out to be simple neglect, not deliberate malfeasance—if, say, the option to purchase the lot for other purposes was about to expire, so a few lies were told or a few palms greased in the 1860s. I had to suppose that there were no Civil War deceased in the town site. Maybe those who still had family members associated with the church had buried them all at Mount Moriah—I'd have to check sometime.

But that wasn't really my problem, was it? Should I go digging through city records to see if there was any more information? From what little I'd read, the city had been rather casual about old cemeteries and hadn't really looked into legal responsibilities, once the church had abandoned their burial ground. Separation of church and state? Or just basic confusion?

James had left after lunch and finally called after six. "You ready to go?"

"My brain has turned to mush, so I guess the answer's yes. Where are you?"

"Downstairs."

"Have you seen Marty or Dylan?"

"No, but I just got here."

"I'll see if I can find them and send them home. This place is closed tomorrow, so we can come back and put in a few more hours. Maybe by then the detective will have sorted out what the police and the city want to do about this mess." Before he could protest, I added, "I know, I know, you have one of those normal day jobs, so you can go to work. We'll manage without you."

"Thank you—I think."

I think one of my feet had gone to sleep, and I sort of stumbled when I stood up. When I could move without limping, I made a quick pass at the map room, and there were Marty and Dylan, working side by side in silence. We were clearly gluttons for punishment, for here we were, hard at work on a weekend.

"Gang," I said, "I can't see straight, and James is waiting for me downstairs. I vote we call it a day and get an early start tomorrow. Marty, you can stay if you want—you've still got a key, right?"

"Yes, but I feel like a zombie. Anything to report?"

"I think I've nailed down the church, although there are still some mysterious elements about what happened to the cemetery. If it wasn't on the up and up, I doubt there will be any records. You?"

"I've been trying to match up the old maps and the 1790 census, plus whatever city directories I can find, but they're kind of patchy. But I'm not done."

"Dylan?" I turned to him.

"I'm kind of new to genealogy, but I think I can put together Ms. Featherstone's history. Tomorrow should do it for a basic outline—or do I mean tree?—and you can tell me which holes I need to fill."

"Excellent work, troops! Does nine o'clock work for you?" When everybody nodded wearily, I added, "Then we're going home. Marty, you want to lock up?"

"Will do. Can we leave everything spread out here?"

"Of course—at least until tomorrow."

When I walked out of the building, the air was cooler—it was a lovely early summer evening in the city. Except that my head was still mired in the eighteenth century. It was so interesting reading about what things had looked like over two hundred years earlier. The cityscape would have been a lot more open, I surmised. I was looking forward to seeing what Marty reconstructed about who lived where. We still weren't any closer to figuring out who that outlying body was, or whose house he'd been buried under. Maybe someone had wanted him to be buried with the others in the big lot across the street but he hadn't been a member of the church or otherwise eligible, and someone had kind of piggybacked the burial, maybe in the dark of night. Or maybe that singleton was not connected at all, and someone had seen a convenient place to hide a body. Maybe the medical examiner could help us. I had a feeling that the man hadn't died of an illness.

"Uh, Nell? Here's where we parked," James's voice broke into my reverie.

I pulled my scattered thoughts back together. "Oh, right. I was trying to visualize this part of the city two centuries ago. You could have seen the river from here, right?"

"Plus a lot of ships. That must have been an amazing sight."

"It's easy to forget Philadelphia was a major port. I've seen enough old maps to know that the docks were stretched out for a good ways along the riverfront, and were fairly close together. I can't imagine maneuvering a sailing ship."

"There weren't many women ship's captains," James commented.

"I'm not surprised. Home?"

"We're running out of food," James pointed out.

"We can shop tomorrow. Tonight I'll settle for scrambled eggs and toast."

"Sounds good to me."

• • •

When I woke up the next morning I realized I was kind of enjoying our shared search to identify the unknown body. How many more might there be under parking lots in the city? Maybe I'd get a local reputation as a Body Hunter, although I was pretty sure that

93

once was enough, and I had a historic library to run. Not to mention the board report to finish, but at least I had a good excuse if it was late.

I wondered if Marty had heard from Barney. I wondered what had happened to Barney, and how he'd feel about what we were in the process of discovering. Apparently bodies were not what he had expected when he planned his apartment building. But I for one was glad that he had reported it, not just covered it all up. Of course, many of his construction workers might have objected to that.

I wandered down to the kitchen to find James dressed and ready to hit the road. "You driving or taking the train?" I asked, and I scrounged up an English muffin.

"If you're ready in less than fifteen minutes we can drive in together."

"I think I can manage that. I don't know if I'll be in the city all day, but I can always get the train back."

"What's your plan for the day?"

"I've identified most of the cemeteries in the immediate vicinity, and I know that a lot of the burials from that batch that Barney found were transferred to Mount Moriah Cemetery. Or at least, that's what the newspaper said at the time. I'm not convinced, and I'm horrified that so many were left behind and nobody noticed. Think there was anything illegal there?"

"Unlikely that anyone left a paper trail, if there was," James commented.

"That's more or less what I thought. Marty said she'd looked at the maps and street listings, such as they were, so we'll go over that today. Dylan was looking into our donor Harriet, both her family ties and the collection she left us. It would be fun to find some more hidden letters and such, but I'm not counting on it—maybe that one we did find was a fluke and doesn't really mean anything. I wish I'd spent more time talking with Harriet—she might have had other secrets. Marty said her mother used to play bridge with Harriet, but that doesn't help much. We already knew she'd lived in Philadelphia all of her life."

James stood up and took his cup and plate to the sink. "You now have six minutes to get dressed."

"Yes, sir! I'm on it!"

Since we were planning to do more grubby work today I didn't bother to dress up, and just threw on a shirt and jeans and hurried downstairs.

As James drove toward the city, he commented, "You seem awfully cheerful for someone who's investigating a city lot full of bodies."

"I don't take it personally, I guess. I don't know any of them, and I probably don't know any of their descendants. So absent any personal connection, it's just a big interesting puzzle. Of course, it bothers me that all those bodies were just forgotten, but at least I can do something about it, in a small way. Marty's body is a bit more complicated, because it was deliberately concealed, so nobody will have left a note saying, 'check out the body under the fifth house from the corner.' And records were a bit patchy then—they could be garbled or lost, or maybe the smaller streets changed names. But if anybody can figure it out, Marty can."

"You think it was a murder?" James asked.

"I'll let the medical examiner decide—there must be some physical evidence, even this long after. But I refuse to believe anyone just stuffed a body under a house in that neighborhood and then just walked away. And nobody's found it since? Except Marty, and finding it scared her into silence for decades."

"You're enjoying this," James stated.

"I am. Is that wrong? We ought to find out who the man was—it seems only right. And it may provide some insight into the history of the city. What's not to like? Don't tell, but it's much more interesting than balancing the Society's budgets and wheedling money out of rich donors."

James dropped me off in front of the Society building and went on his way to his job, where he did serious, important things. I had to smile at my own comment then: I was doing similar things—finding bodies, solving what may have been crimes—if in a slightly less serious vein. I had nothing to apologize for.

Marty was sitting on the steps. "Waiting for me?" I asked, dropping down next to her.

"Just enjoying the weather. I almost wish it would rain—I could get more work done that way."

"True. But think of the mess it would make of the old cemetery. Any word from Barney?"

"The answer is still no. Maybe he decided to do some more exploring on his own and a building fell on him. Or maybe he's a fake and doesn't have any rights to the property at all. Or maybe he's a treasure hunter looking for antique jewelry in the old cemetery. Or maybe he's a crazy genealogist hoping to find his eighteenth-century family members."

"Stop," I protested. "Can't we assume he's exactly what he appears to be? He's an ordinary guy."

"Sure. Fine," Marty grumbled. "I've known of him for years, but not well. I could show you other buildings in the city that his company has built. It's not large—I mean, he can't compete with people building skyscrapers around here—but he does good work, and delivers on time. I want to believe he was as surprised as anyone by what he found at the site. And if we don't get things figured out, he's going to lose money waiting."

"Hey," I protested. "I've got nothing against him. I just wondered why he seems to have disappeared at this particular time."

Marty sighed. "I don't know."

"You have anything good to share from your research yesterday?"

"I do, or at least a start. You?"

"I told you, I've got the church nailed down, I think, although I'd like to see what your maps show. There's a bit of a mystery involved, but it's more about why these particular bodies got left behind than about who they are. And the church has been through so many changes that I doubt anybody knows what happened. Plus, I doubt it has anything to do with your body. I hope I didn't overwhelm Dylan—he's never claimed to be a genealogist, and he hasn't worked in a place like this, so I hope I didn't ask too much from him."

"He's a smart kid, and he seems to like this kind of work. The two of us can't handle all the details, particularly not on a short schedule, so it's good that we have Dylan to help. You ready to go in?"

"I am. I want to see how all our pieces fit together. And we may hear from Detective Hrivnak today, so I'd like to be able to give her some answers."

Marty stood up and waited for me to stand. "Lead the way. I want answers too."

Chapter Fourteen

I let us in and locked the door behind us. If Dylan hadn't already come in, he had a key, so he could let himself in. Marty and I headed straight for the map room, and yes, Dylan was already there. Marty had left the materials she'd collected scattered on one of the big tables, so we were ready to get to work.

"Hi, Dylan," I greeted him. "How's it going?"

"It's coming along. I'm trying not to get too excited before I show you what I've got."

"That's fine. As I told Marty, I expect to hear from Detective Hrivnak sometime today—she's usually pretty good about keeping us in the loop, and I'm sure all of us want to see this whole thing cleared up quickly, so Barney's construction can move forward."

"Nobody's going to argue to turn the land into a cemetery again?" Dylan asked.

"That seems pretty unlikely, and from what I was reading yesterday, if the city or a church did that for one site, there are apparently a whole lot of other buried cemeteries in the city that might lobby for equal treatment. Let me start at the beginning and lay out what I know."

I proceeded to outline what I'd found the day before, ending with my bewilderment that some of the burials had been moved, apparently publicly, but a lot more had not. While I talked, Marty had pulled out a modern map of Philadelphia and laid it in the center of the table between us.

"Let me get this straight," Marty began. "You said that our cemetery—or maybe it's Barney's—was opened in 1707, right? And there was a Baptist church to go with it."

"Yes, that's what I found," I told her.

"And the church moved or changed hands or was remodeled or merged with other churches for the next hundred and fifty years?"

"Yes. I don't think we need to collect all the details, unless the police or the city want to know who might be responsible for the bodies now."

Marty snorted. "I wish them luck with that! Anyway, Nell, you said that in 1860—right at the beginning of the Civil War?—whichever church it was then decided to move the whole cemetery. Do you happen to know if they sold the land outright, or the city seized it?"

"I didn't see anything about that in the sources I found, but I can keep looking. Anyway, officially the cemetery was relocated in part of the existing Mount Moriah Cemetery, which was already established. That was well south of our cemetery. What's funny is that the public announcement suggested that people who already had plots could either move their loved ones to Mount Moriah or could pick up the burials and take them elsewhere. Hard to imagine, isn't it?"

"How many made it to Mount Moriah?" Marty asked.

"I don't know. I've looked at a Google map, but the plot whose number I have doesn't look big enough to accommodate hundreds of burials. Or maybe they took only those whose owners were willing to pay. But they might have better records from the nineteenth century. Before you ask, I haven't found any church records listing who was buried and where, but I've only been looking for a day."

"You think what happened was legal?" Dylan asked.

"You mean, leaving all those bodies behind? I have no idea," I told him. "And I didn't notice any tombstones lying around on that lot, although there were some pretty complete coffins, so it seems unlikely that the bodies were just dumped there. Did the Baptists use grave markers? I know the Quakers are pretty low-key about them."

"I didn't see any either," Dylan agreed. "You think whoever took the place apart in the nineteenth century might have reused the stones for, like, building material? Foundations?"

"Interesting idea. Let's make a note of that and save it for later. You know, if we keep finding things like this, we may mess up property values in that part of town. Anyway, right now I don't know anything more. The authorities may have something to add, like who's responsible for clearing the ground. Marty, you want to tell us what you've got?"

"You asked me to try to find who owned the house where I found that body. It was vacant when I saw it, and it looks vacant now. Hard to believe, isn't it? A house standing empty in that neighborhood for so long? Anyway, I started by looking at the 1790 census. Have you ever looked at that, Nell?" When I shook my head, she continued, "It's really interesting, and it's available online. The writing is very clear, and there's lots of detail. It's divided into columns that list the name of the occupant, which mostly meant heads of families, then the profession of the occupant, how many people lived or worked in the building, whether it was a house or a store, and then the last columns break down the occupants by gender. And the final one is for slaves. And cemeteries are listed, although they don't count how many people are buried. And there are also listings for both vacant lots and vacant houses."

"Wow," I said. "I really should have looked at this at some point— it sounds fascinating. But does this help us?"

"Maybe. The most useful thing I found was a listing for the dwelling at the corner of Second Street, on the west side—that's the side the cemetery was on. It was a mixed neighborhood, with a lot of different professions listed, but the important one for us was that corner lot, which belonged to William Young, who was a printer— and a bookbinder." Marty sat back and waited for our reaction.

Dylan perked up immediately. "William Young? *The* William Young?"

"You know about him?" Marty asked with a half smile.

"Hey, guys, fill me in, please," I protested.

"And you work in a library, Nell?" Dylan said in a tone of mock horror. "He was one of the first great printers in Philadelphia history. I'll bet you have some of his work here at the Society."

"And at the Library Company," Marty added.

"Okay, he was a big name. And we know he was in business there in 1790. What does that tell us?"

"His shop—which must have been rather crowded, because the census lists five males over sixteen, two under sixteen, six free white females, and one 'other'—makes you wonder what an 'other' was in those days. And we found a document that was added to the binding of a book—or maybe I should say rebinding. All right, maybe another coincidence—but we're running into a lot of those."

"Didn't Young train apprentices, or were all these his family?" Dylan asked. "Either way, somebody in that household could have done it."

"Hold on! Where was this corner house in relation to the house with your body, Marty?" I asked.

"A couple of doors south, on the same block."

"And I've got another piece of the puzzle," Dylan announced triumphantly. "I sketched out Harriet Featherstone's family tree—nothing fancy, and not too much detail—but I'm pretty sure her family at the end of the eighteenth century lived on the same block. I'd need to do some more digging, but like Marty said, this is another coincidence. Maybe the house with the body was her family's back then—maybe one of the ones that was vacant then so nobody was living in it. Or they rented it out. Marty, did people rent out houses back then?"

"Sometimes," Marty told him, "though renters might not have been included in the census—I'd have to check that. Look, we've got a lot of suggestive details, and they kind of fit together, but I've still got a lot of questions, and I want to check the details before I tell anyone official. Like our detective friend."

"Believe me, I understand," I said. "And so will she—she wants facts, not wild guesses. That goes for all of us. But it does make a great story. Thank you both."

"What do we do now?" Dylan asked. "Do you want us to keep looking?"

"Actually I'd like to hear what Detective Hrivnak wants to do next. She may not be interested in this stuff and I don't want to waste our time, unless you're interested for yourselves, not the law."

I almost jumped when my cell phone rang, especially when I saw who it was: the detective. These coincidences were really piling up. I answered quickly. "Good morning, Detective. What can I do for you?"

"You in the city? If you are, get yourself over here to the building lot—there's something you've got to see."

"We can be there in a few minutes." We hung up at the same time.

Marty and Dylan were staring at me. "What?" Marty demanded.

"She wants us to see something over near the cemetery. That's all she said."

"Then let's go!"

It took us a couple of minutes to collect what we thought we might need for this unidentified thing that Detective Hrivnak thought we needed to see ASAP. I made sure we took a camera, if the police would let us use it. I tried to imagine what would get her so worked up, but there were too many choices. At least she was including us—or me, at least. She didn't know I had the rest of my small crew with me, and no way was I going to leave them behind.

After another few minutes we arrived at the construction site, only slightly breathless. To my surprise, she waved us over toward the house on the street, which I kept thinking of as Marty's house. We met in front of it.

Things had changed since we'd last seen it. Apparently the police had decided to deal with the body under the house, and the gaping hole in the foundation had been shored up with wood and metal supports. Now it looked as though an adult could actually crawl into it without worrying that the whole building would fall on his or her head.

"Thanks for the call," I told the detective. "Remind me later that we've been collecting information about this site that might be helpful to you. What did you want us to see?"

Detective Hrivnak seemed to be looking at Marty. "You told us when you were a kid you saw a body inside here."

"That's right. Scared me to death."

"Was there only one?"

"That's all I saw, but I got out of there fast."

"Did you see anything else unexpected?"

"No. One body, which was mostly a skeleton by then, was plenty. I never came back. Why are you asking?"

"You missed a few things. Take a look inside—don't worry, we reinforced it. Here—take my flashlight."

Marty gave her a dubious look, but then she approached the hole in the wall. She bent low and scuttled in, flashlight lit. For a minute or two she was silent, and then she said, "Holy crap."

"What's going on?" I demanded.

"You'll get your chance," Marty said, her voice echoing. So we waited.

It was another couple of minutes before Marty crawled out again. I tried to read her expression, but it was a weird mix of surprise and confusion and I didn't know what. "What is it?" I demanded.

She handed me the flashlight. "You've got to see this yourself."

Since she wasn't sharing, I grabbed the flashlight and dove in, cautiously. The body that we knew about—the one we had seen from Dylan's pictures—was about five feet in, but now I could tell there was more. But I couldn't quite believe my eyes. The first body, or what was left of him, lay with its head toward the opening, no surprise. But with the brighter light I could see that there was a *second* body, lying parallel to the first, and slightly to the rear of it. Male, and from what little evidence there was, about the same age and build as the first one. Okay, that was interesting, but I'd have to digest it, and we definitely needed more and better pictures.

I raised the flashlight toward the rear of the hole under the building, which seemed to go back quite a ways. And then I froze. There, a few feet behind the two bodies on the ground, was what looked like a substantial stack of . . . cannons? What the heck was a batch of cannons doing under an old building here? I knew next to nothing about artillery from any era, but to my unskilled eye they looked fairly large, and they were shiny brass rather than cast iron and appeared to be in good condition. *Oh my.* I had no idea what this meant, but I knew I wanted to find out. I was sorely tempted to sit down and study this unexpected find, but I also wanted some answers, so reluctantly I backed out, stood up, brushed off my jeans, and demanded, "What the heck? Were those what I think they are?"

Detective Hrivnak grinned. "You bet."

"Old? Authentic?" I continued.

"Looks like it. I thought maybe you could help us figure this out. You've gotta know more than I do."

"Hey," Dylan interrupted, "do I get to see too?"

"Here." I handed him the flashlight. "Go for it."

He disappeared into the hole.

I shook my head to clear it, not that it helped much. I turned back to the detective. "First, let me thank you for showing this to us. Has the medical examiner had a chance to see the bodies?"

"Nope. He's kind of busy. By the way, the current body count is around four hundred dead."

I hadn't expected that. "Seriously?"

"Yup," Hrivnak replied.

"Well, for us that's a good thing that the medical examiner hadn't gotten to them yet. Can I ask you not to disturb the bodies until we've examined the whole site? Wait—did your people go back any farther or is this all there is?"

"We stabilized the ceiling. There may be more behind, but it's not passable yet—the ceiling fell at some point."

"Okay, Marty? Do you know anyone who would like to help us?"

Marty looked as though her mind was a few thousand miles away, so it took a moment for her to focus. "You mean, like a historical archeologist? Sure, I'll make some phone calls."

Back to Hrivnak. "Do you have a deadline? I doubt we'll bring out a herd of people with toothbrushes and dental picks, but I'd prefer you wouldn't send in a crew with pickaxes and destroy whatever evidence there might be. If any. I think these guys have been here a long time."

"Don't worry," she replied. "I think we've got enough to do with the others over there in the onetime cemetery."

And I might be the only person who knew where they'd come from, but I'd be happy to share that information with her.

Dylan crawled out from the hole. He looked like someone had given him a wonderful Christmas gift. "Wow," he said reverently.

"My sentiments exactly," I told him. "Detective, are you planning to jump into this today, or do you have to get permissions and clearances or some more heavy equipment in first?"

"The second one. Why?"

"Because I'd like some time to think about this and look up a few things."

"You can have the rest of today, but we might get started as early as tomorrow morning."

"No problem," I said firmly. Which was ridiculous if I hoped to get anything accomplished, but I wasn't about to let this opportunity get away.

I turned to look at my companions. Both of them looked kind of shell-shocked, and I wondered if I looked the same. I had not been expecting to find what we found. Marty was at least somewhat prepared, but she'd been looking for only one body, and now we had two, and cannons. Cannons! Where had they come from? What were they doing where they'd been found? They looked to be in pretty good shape, but what did I know? Were they real? Antique or modern? Maybe the two dead men had been dressed up for some sort of reenactment and something had gone very wrong. That was way beyond my expertise to evaluate, but I could certainly do some research on cannons. And in a city so steeped in history, surely there'd be some experts who would be happy to fill us in.

"The new museum," Marty said suddenly, and I wondered if she'd been reading my mind.

"What?" I asked, confused.

"You know, the one that just opened a couple of years ago. The one with the tent. There's a lot of overlap with the Society's board and theirs, and if that administration doesn't know cannons, I can't think of anyone else in the city who would."

"Are you saying the three of us should or shouldn't do some research of our own?"

"Oh, sure, we can go ahead—we've probably got plenty of records. But it would be faster and more efficient to work with people who know a bit more. Let them look at the weapons side. We can still add our parts about the neighborhood and the church, because those have to fit with leaving the cannons there. And the deaths of two men who didn't belong to the cemetery. Did they live in that neighborhood, or were they just dumped there?"

"There's no history of commemorating a burial with a few spare weapons?" I asked dubiously.

"I sincerely doubt it."

"Well, I may not know much about how to make a cannon, but I'm pretty sure they're heavy, so it's unlikely a group of people would just wander in and park a cannon, much less a whole batch of cannons. Unless it was a large group of people, and you'd think there'd be a record of something like that."

I thought for a moment. "Okay, then. So we go back to the Society and do some more investigation. I'm going to check again for information about the church and its members, and maybe Mount Moriah if I have time. Dylan, you've probably still got a lot to do with Harriet's gift and any personal information you can find about her. How close to finished are you?"

"Hard to say," Dylan answered. "I think I've found all the new pieces from her collection, but I've been looking carefully at each book to see if it's been altered, which slows things down. Knowing that William Young might have had a hand in binding them, or rebinding them, makes it more exciting, but if that's true, it would be a shame to take the books apart hoping to find something else. At least we know when he was in business."

"Good. Marty?"

"If I have time I'm going to look into cannons. I've met Harold Stevens at the museum, so I'll give him a call and ask if he wants to get involved. But there is one practical matter to talk about. We were kind of first on the scene, by invitation, when they found the bodies. I'd like to keep the Society front and center publicly, say, if the press wants us to report. We know we aren't the experts in a lot of these areas, like how to date the bodies or figuring out when the cannons were made and if they were stashed at the same time as the bodies, but we represent the Society, and we need to use that for our own selfish reasons. Like, stay ahead of the story, and make sure the public knows the police came to us first. Can you handle that, Nell?"

"I'd better be able to! You have any friends at the *Inquirer*?"

"I've got a few names. I'll pass them on to you. But we'd better get on it today, or somebody else will grab the attention."

"I get your point. But even if we figure out who was buried in the cemetery and what happened, I'd rather run with identifying the two men with the cannons. I wonder if James knows any FBI medical folk. Not that I want to tick off the city's person, but he's got a lot of bodies on his hands, even if he doesn't spend much time with each of them."

"Okay, okay," Marty said impatiently. "Look, I know you've got a full-time job, so you can't just veer off and do something else, no matter how interesting it is. But you can use whatever you find to promote the Society, and it is relevant to your mission. Just don't get carried away. Find enough details to make a good story, and then let the experts take over. If you rough out the story quickly, I can get it to the right people."

"Thanks for the reality check, Marty. But that applies to all of us—a bit of church history, a dash of genealogy, and some insight about the neighborhoods back in the eighteenth century. Something for everyone. And as you reminded me, don't get caught up in a tangent just because it's interesting. If people want more, they can come looking for us. Can we get this together by the end of the day?"

"Yes," Marty said. "So let's go."

We split up and went to our separate corners. I sat down at my desk and tried to decide where to start. I turned on my computer and opened our electronic card catalogue, listing all the Society's documents and books, and the first thing I came up with was a guide to the gravestone inscriptions for the lost cemetery. Duh. How had I missed it yesterday? I wrote down the call number and trekked to the stacks. When I found it I sat down on a stool and skimmed it. As near as I could see, it did account for some or all of the removals to Mount Moriah, but for the Center City burials only names were given, not where within the cemetery they had been buried. Still, it was a start, and it might be helpful to the police or the medical examiner.

And there I stopped. I was sure there was more information buried in some library somewhere, but did we need it now? I'd put together the basic outline of what had happened, but this was a police investigation, not a social history. I'd probably collected enough to keep most people happy. So now what?

I had to admit that two dead men and a stack of old cannons was more interesting than a few hundred skeletons when we knew why they were where they were, even if we couldn't put names to them. So I should turn back to the two mystery men and the cannons. How old were those cannons? Where did they come from? And why were they under a building?

In a totally irreverent thought, I reminded myself that I shouldn't publicize that the city was built on who knew how many dead bodies—it might discourage tourism, or alternately, suggest that tourists should come equipped with shovels and do some digging of their own. Some people might find that creepy, but others would probably be excited by the idea.

Where to start? Surely we would have some information on metal casting at the Society. That would take a forge, right? Something to melt the metal before molding it? I understood that there had been quite a few around Philadelphia—including Valley Forge, which was probably the best known by outsiders. Then there was the question of where the raw materials had come from. I also happened to know that there were several important mines in Pennsylvania, since we had some members who were descended from the mine owners, but I wasn't sure that would help, beyond proving that the materials would have been available early on.

How one actually went about putting together a cannon was another issue, and there I'd need help. And of course, cannons needed wheels or carriages or something just to move them from one place to another. There would have been some sort of wheels in that hole under the house, but it seemed improbable that there would have been enough of them to move the number of cannons we'd seen. Which I speculated might have meant that the cannons were not battle-ready, but they were being transported from one place to another before whatever battle they were intended for. What's more, I was pretty sure that a quick examination of the cannons themselves would probably show whether they had been used or were new.

I was beginning to think that calling in the weapons expert sooner rather than later would be a good idea. We needed to date the cannons, and find out if they'd ever been used. And where would this person want to examine them? Surely not under the house. At police HQ, or at his own home base? Or even at the Society? It might be fun for people to see them up close and personal, in their original state, not all polished up and pretty. But we'd divested ourselves of physical collections at the Society, in favor of books and other printed materials, so it probably wouldn't work.

I fished out my mobile phone and called Marty, who I knew was still in the building. When she picked up she sounded preoccupied. "What?" she barked.

"I've been thinking—maybe we should talk to your weapons expert sooner rather than later. That should give us some dates and a point or points of origin. Where would he want to work on them? I can call the detective and confirm whether they'll be ready to remove the bodies and the cannons tomorrow, and where they will put them."

"Good point. But we should also think about where they're going to end up. If we all wait for someone at the city to determine who the original owner was, we could be waiting a long time. Better get it settled now."

"I agree. You want to make the call?"

"Sure, no problem."

After Marty hung up, I decided I should look up a few details about cannons—or refresh my memory at least, since I'd read up on them a bit when I'd been looking at the story of the Battle of Paoli, out in the suburbs. That was why I knew they had to be moved on wheels—which had failed miserably when the Americans had tried to get out of Paoli in the middle of the night. But I didn't know much about the range of sizes for cannons, and what size shot they took, and what each size was intended for. Or how to make them, for that matter. I knew one when I saw one—a cylinder with a hole in it. Ammo went in the back end and came out the front end. And that was all.

So I pulled together a sample of documents and a book or two and started reading. In what era should I start? I collected facts along the way. In the later eighteenth century, there weren't a lot of foundries in the colonies, but the Continental Army needed the big guns—that was their main weapon. They were made of bronze and steel, but steel was stronger. The French had helped out by providing some of the metal. The shot and cannonballs used could travel as far as two miles, but the average range for cannons was one to two thousand yards. And, yes, I'd been right: they needed the carriage to move the things around. Cannon types included field guns, which were mobile, and siege guns, which were bigger and heavier. There were also mortars and howitzers.

I decided to ignore the last two models: I knew what I had seen were cannons. They had been expensive to make, as was the gunpowder that fueled them. The basic model, which was the most often used for a couple of centuries, was made of cast iron or bronze, with a cartridge of gunpowder, and a projectile. When fired (apparently lit by a tube filled with gunpowder), it had a wicked recoil and had to be dragged back into firing position by the gun crew.

I decided I'd read enough. I wasn't sure I needed to know what they shot, only that they could fire something. In other words, they weren't anybody's pretty garden ornament. The big ones were unwieldy and hard to move, and then you had to think about moving the ammunition as well. They came in a lot of different sizes, and the cannonballs ranged from three pounds to twenty-four pounds. I came across one reference that said that in 1776 sixty twelve-pounders and eighteen-pounders were cast in Pennsylvania.

By now I realized that my education in military history had been pathetic. Most of this information I had never thought of. Sure, I'd seen cannons, in battlefield parks or city monuments, but I'd never considered how they worked. But I'd been a girl, and we weren't supposed to care about things like that. Yet here I was, trying to figure out what the things under the abandoned house had been, how old they were, and why they were there. Had anyone ever gone looking for them? Had they been deliberately hidden or just dumped? Were they intact or broken?

I gave up. I knew just barely enough to talk about the things without sounding like an idiot, but I would never manage to learn all these details, nor did I really need to, because there were people in the city who could tell me what I needed to know. I'd wait for Marty's call and see if she'd found us an expert.

As if by magic, my phone rang at that moment. It was Marty. Without preamble she said, "Harold is on his way over to the construction site. He'll meet us there."

"Huh? Wait—who's Harold?"

"Harold Stevens. He's on the board of that Revolution museum. Have you heard anything from the detective?"

"About what?"

"Getting the bodies and the cannons out of the hole."

"No. We can sort it out when we get there. I hope Harold isn't fussy about dirt."

Chapter Fifteen

I found Marty and Dylan waiting impatiently downstairs in the lobby. "What's the story on this guy Harold, Marty?"

"He's on the museum board, along with a lot of other people, many of whom you probably know. He's their artillery specialist. You know those cannons out in front of the building?" When I nodded—I had a vague memory of walking past them—she went on, "He was responsible for finding them, authenticating them, and persuading the rest of the board to install them front and center. You should know that if you walk around Philadelphia a lot, you'll see other cannons here and there."

"I'd bet people found them too heavy to move and just left them where they found them. We'd better get going. I take it we're going to let Harold see the cannons?"

"I hope so. Of course, Detective Hrivnak will have to get the bodies out first, and I'm sure she can't wait to show them to us."

"I hope Harold brought a photographer, or we may lose evidence."

"We've told her about six times to preserve the setup and any artifacts she finds. Let's hope she was listening."

"I'll let her do what she wants with the other couple of hundred," Marty said glumly.

We set off briskly and arrived less than ten minutes later. Marty waved, and a guy I had to assume was Harold waved back to her. He was younger than I had expected—but why did I assume board members were grizzled old men? (Probably because they were the ones with money to donate, I reminded myself.) When I got closer I realized he did look kind of familiar, so I probably had met him before at a Society event. Detective Hrivnak stood behind him, looking like smoke was coming out of her ears.

"I haven't touched anything, so you archeology types can stop worrying," she said. "Can we just get this over with?"

Harold ignored the detective and turned to me. "I understand you've got two bodies in front of an unknown number of cannons, under a building?" Harold asked eagerly. "Any ideas about the dates?"

"Yes about the bodies," Marty said, "and no clue about how old they are. I figured you'd want to see the bodies first, before you looked at all the artillery. You might notice something we wouldn't."

I thought Marty's comment was an understatement, but I didn't say anything.

"Are the bodies wearing uniforms?" Harold asked.

"I don't think we've gotten close enough to tell," Hrivnak said.

"How long does cloth survive under the circumstances?" I followed up quickly.

By now we were standing in front of the shored-up foundation. Harold studied it, poked a toe at the ground, and sniffed. "Since this is close to the waterfront, I'd assume it's always sort of damp, which wouldn't be good for natural fabrics. Don't count on finding much, unless we get lucky and find some metal buttons or something."

"What shape are the bodies in, Detective?" he went on.

"Nell, you've seen more of them than I have. What's your take?"

"Well, the bodies were identifiable as human bodies, though there wasn't much flesh left," I said after thinking for a moment. "All the pieces were in the right order, not like they'd been ripped apart by animals or even dissected by another human. There were enough shreds of cloth to identify them as clothed. And I'm not even going to guess how old the bodies are or how long they've been laying here."

"I can help you with that," Harold volunteered.

"Good," the detective said. She gestured over to a couple of guys standing by a couple of gurneys, waiting for us to finish. "Guys? Let's get this started," she called out.

They approached and entered the hole carefully. I checked off one more area of expertise that I was lacking: moving old bodies. I didn't think I could handle it if one fell apart in my hands.

Marty, Dylan and I stepped back and watched from a respectful distance. Harold was more eager and got as close as he could. The work didn't progress very fast, but I assume jostling the remains would mean we might lose important evidence. I tried to remember the history of money in Philadelphia, in case there were coins in the pockets of the dead men, but came up blank.

It didn't take long for the first man to emerge from the hole, and the coroner's people, or whoever they were, laid him out carefully on a gurney, without losing any bits and pieces. I was less disgusted than I expected (thanks to watching a lot of crime shows)—what I felt was mainly curiosity.

The detective was eyeing me, probably wondering what I would do next. "Can I get closer?" I asked.

"I don't think you can do any harm at this point. Just don't touch," she responded.

Marty was looking kind of pale. She gave Harold a push and said, "Go ahead, check it—him?—out."

"Thanks," he said quickly, and moved to stand beside me. We stood and stared for a couple of minutes. My quick assessment was that yes, he was male, with a surprising amount of leathery-looking flesh still attached; he wasn't particularly tall, maybe my height; he was wearing some remnants of clothes that looked handmade, but I could have been wrong. Still, I was pretty sure they predated commercial sewing machines. He still had most of his teeth. I hesitated to guess at the cause of death, but I didn't see anything that looked like a bullet hole. So maybe he died in a fight? "Harold, what do you think?" I finally asked.

"Hard to say," Harold replied, his gaze never leaving the remains. "Maybe a particularly strong blow, or a stab wound, which wouldn't be obvious in his condition now. No uniform. No apparent personal weapon, although it could still be further in the hole or it was buried under the body. I'm not much help, I'm afraid."

I looked around for Marty, who seemed to be retreating. She really must have been upset by finding the body as a child and never quite gotten over it. "Anything to add, Marty? Is this the man you remember?"

"I'm no scientist. He's a skeleton, but he looks like he's been dead for a long time. That's all I can say."

"Ready for the second one?" Detective Hrivnak asked. When we all nodded, she gestured to the gurney guys to wheel away the first man and retrieve the second. That took another couple of minutes, since there was less room to maneuver farther back inside the hole. Finally the second man emerged into the sunshine, and Harold and I crept closer again, followed by Dylan.

I decided that to my eyes a skeleton was a skeleton, period. This one looked to be about the same size as the first man, but if he was no more than a couple of inches taller or shorter I couldn't say. But, I realized, there was something different about this man: what was left of his clothes was more substantial than that of the first man's, and he was wearing boots. And Harold certainly looked more excited now. He looked over at Detective Hrivnak. "May I touch him?"

After a moment she nodded. Harold approached the body carefully, then reached out for something on its chest, though I couldn't see what it was. When he withdrew his hand, he was holding something small and round and grayish. He laid it carefully on the open palm of his other hand. "It's a button," he said reverently.

I came closer and peered at it. "Metal. Is it military, do you think?"

Harold nodded. "What insignia do you see?" He held it out toward me.

I looked more closely, and then despite the corrosion the image came together for me. "It's a crown."

"Exactly. It's British, or at least Loyalist—those folks who remained loyal to England, at least up until the war."

"So that gives us a date," I said, almost to myself. "Can you date it?"

"I'd have to check some sources, but I think it's safe to say that it's from the 1770s."

"And the man wasn't wearing a really old coat?"

"If he'd been American he would have changed the buttons."

Detective Hrivnak's voice cut into our quiet conversation. "You guys about done? Because we've still got the cannons to dig out."

And, I reminded myself, there could be more interesting souvenirs scattered around inside the hole. Harold asked politely, "Detective, may I keep this button and do some more research? I'll give you a receipt if you want."

"Sure, fine," she said—clearly she didn't think it was very important. She turned to the gurney guys. "You, take the bodies back to the ME's office. He's expecting them. But treat them carefully—too much banging around and you'll end up with a pile of bones." The men took hold of the first gurney and trundled off toward a waiting van at the curb.

While the detective organized the delivery of the bodies, Harold, Marty, Dylan, and I stood there looking shell-shocked. I wasn't sure what to think, and we didn't have a lot of facts to work with. On the recent end, Marty had seen the nearer body nearly half a century ago, but I couldn't begin to guess how long it took a body to deteriorate to its present condition. On the earlier end, Harold believed the button he had found on one of the bodies dated to the era of the Revolutionary War. It had still been attached to what was left of the body's clothing. Which could mean that the body too dated to the Revolution, which was not particularly unlikely for this end of the city.

But where did the cannons fit in this picture? And why were there two men dead, and why had they been left in this location? We had a few answers, but a lot more questions.

"Ready for the cannons?" Detective Hrivnak asked loudly.

"Should we rummage around the space first?" I asked.

Harold answered quickly. "Won't make that much difference, Nell. You can do the sifting after they're out of the way."

"How much do these things weigh?" the detective asked him.

"Depends on the size, and that's hard to guess right now," Harold told her. "Could be a thousand pounds or even more. Each. Do you have a plan for moving them?"

"I think somebody said something about a winch. Let me check." She strode across the street to confer with some of her team.

"Harold, do you have any ideas?" I asked while she was gone.

"About what happened here? I've got some guesses, but I wouldn't put money on them. It's great that the detective will give us access to them."

"Do you need a lab or something?" Dylan asked. "I could probably get permission to use one at the university, if you tell me what you need."

"Thanks, Dylan, but I need to get a general handle on what we're looking at before I get into details."

"Do you think the bodies and the artillery are as old as they look?"

"I won't say no. They're definitely not modern, and most likely not Civil War."

I looked up to see the missing Barney approaching—on crutches, one leg wrapped in a cast. "Hi, guys!" he called out. "Looks like I've been missing all the fun. The detective lady said you all were over here. What's up?"

"Barney, what happened to you? You just disappeared in the middle of the first time we were here, and we haven't heard from you since. We were worried about you!"

He grinned briefly. "Bet you thought I'd joined the dead guys across the street." The smile left his face as he grimaced. "Damn, this hurts. I knew the crew wouldn't be here because of the police investigation, but it never occurred to me to call you all. Sorry."

"Where'd you go?" I asked.

"I'd arranged to meet a supplier that afternoon. I thought it would be a quick meeting and I'd be back, but he wanted to talk, I wanted a good price from him, so time got away from me. Plus we were in a pub, a couple of streets over, and we had a few beers, and maybe a few more. He finally left, and I figured you all would have gone home by then. So I was coming out of the pub and missed a step and landed funny, and it turns out I tore a ligament or something in my ankle. I thought I could walk it off, but it kept getting worse, so I took myself to the ER. I had to wait hours, since I wasn't bleeding or having a heart attack, and it was real late by the time they patched me up. With some good pharmaceuticals, I might add, which knocked me out once I got home. I wish I'd stayed here with you all. You've found out something new?"

"For heaven's sake, Barney," Marty interrupted, "let's find a place to sit down and we'll fill you in."

"Thanks, Marty. Who's this?" He was looking at Harold.

"He works for the new Revolution museum," I told him. "You'll see why he's here when we've explained what we found." Obviously there were no convenient benches along the street, but we found a piece of concrete wall that Barney could sit on while we filled him in.

"You know by now that the police are involved, because you've got a lot of bodies here, and Detective Hrivnak has been running the show," I began. "Marty and I have worked with her before, so we got lucky. Marty, Dylan and I have been doing some research at the Society, and since you were here we've figured out what church this cemetery belonged to, and we may even have a listing of who was buried here. But I haven't shared it with the police yet, and I think they should hear it first. But the most interesting thing is that there were two bodies found under a house across the street from the rest. I'll let Marty tell you about them."

"Great. Marty, I'm all ears."

Marty ran through what we already knew about her finding a

body years ago, and our snooping after that, and then the research we'd managed to do since, up until this morning. Barney just kept saying "Wow!"

Finally Marty ran out of steam. "Barney, you own the land that we now know was a cemetery, right?"

"I've got an option on it, and I've put money down, but it's not mine until the building goes up and I can sell the units."

Marty nodded. "And you told me you'd gotten all the permits and any other documents?"

"Sure did," he said. "I didn't want to run into any problems. Time is money in this business. Guess that didn't quite work out as planned. So what did you find on the east side of the street? Which I have no claim to, by the way."

"Those two bodies and a pile of cannons," Harold said.

It was almost comic to watch Barney's chin drop in surprise, I thought. "Cannons? Here?" Barney said.

Marty responded, "Yup. We haven't counted them yet—the bodies were in front of them and we wanted to get them cleared out. They're on their way to the ME's office. When Hrivnak gets back she wants to go in after the cannons. She's looking for some equipment to do it."

"Wow," Barney said again, reverently. "How many you think there are?"

"Hard to say right now, since it's dark in there and we don't know how far back they go. But more than just a couple."

"Man, am I glad that I came back in time to see this!"

"Barney, you don't happen to know who owns or used to own any of the properties on this side?" I asked.

"I didn't worry about them because I didn't need them. Does it matter?"

"We just wondered if anybody would have a claim to the cannons. Otherwise I'm pretty sure Harold here will snatch them up for his museum."

"I assume you museum people are looking into the ownership side?" Barney asked.

"Of course," I said quickly. "We've already started. In this case we know more than the police do."

"Well, I'm not going to worry about it. The only thing that bothers me is that there might be tenants who aren't happy living over what was a cemetery, even if all the bodies are gone."

I smiled a bit grimly. "This is Philadelphia. It may take a while to sort out what to do with them. But we're sharing everything we find, so I hope that helps."

Chapter Sixteen

Once the bodies had been dispatched, Detective Hrivnak returned. "So, you made it back, Mr. Taylor. How's the leg?"

"It's okay, but I don't think I'll be doing much digging in the near future. Still, I couldn't stay away from all this." He waved his hand over the dirt plot, which to my eyes looked as though it had been invaded by giant gophers. "Or the extras on this side," Barney added.

The detective went on, "Just to be clear, you have no claim to the east side of the street? Your property ends with the cemetery plot?"

"That's what I understand. Believe me, I went through it all with the city and my lawyers back when I started planning this."

"Did they tell you who it did belong to?"

"If they mentioned it, it didn't mean anything to me. I didn't need that section. Still, it's part of the history of this neighborhood, so I figured I'd better know as much as I could. Mind if I watch?"

"Just keep out of the way. I think we've figured out how to move the cannons."

"How many people will it take?" I asked, merely out of curiosity.

"Maybe three or four each? You might be able to tell me how they did it in the old days."

"Two-wheeled carriages," Harold answered promptly. "I don't suppose you have any horses to spare."

"Not likely," the detective answered.

"Well, all I ask is that you try not to bang them up too much. From what little I can see, the cannons look like they've never been used and they're in great condition."

"I'll let you tell me if that's true, once we get them out in the open."

It took nearly half an hour to find the right equipment, and some ropes that would be strong enough to move around half a ton of metal, and a place to lay them that didn't involve dragging them over rocky soil and chunks of paving and scratching them up. Harold kept hovering like a mother hen—he was really excited by our find. Some of the police workers inspected the shoring timbers of the space beneath the building, so that we could be sure that the roof or the rest of the building wouldn't fall on anyone's head—we didn't need a fatality on the site now, and I was pretty sure the city didn't need a lawsuit from us.

And then the hauling of the cannons started, slowly. I hoped Dylan was getting pictures of it—I hadn't noticed any reporters with cameras on the scene. It took the better part of thirty minutes to move each cannon, and as they emerged each appeared to be about six feet long. That was a lot of metal. The pile of them grew slowly until it was about a dozen cannons of the same size and configuration. And decoration, too, although I wasn't standing close enough to decipher it.

One officer was standing in front of the hole, shaking his head, as the twelfth cannon joined its mates. "You about done?" Hrivnak called out.

"I don't think so. Come take a look."

For some reason we all moved like a herd to look into the dark hole. Which didn't look as dark anymore, and not because the sun was at our backs.

"Is that a tunnel?" I asked incredulously.

"Looks like it, except the far end fell in a while ago."

I had thought the Philadelphia tunnels were urban legends. Or abandoned subway tunnels. Or tourist attractions. "Does it go as far as the river?"

Harold seemed to have perked up again now that he'd absorbed what he was seeing. "Might have, once upon a time. But there's been so much construction between here and there that it might be hard to prove it."

"But think about it," I told him. "Here we have a batch of big cannons, and each one had to be heavy. Who the heck was going to drag them through city streets without getting a lot of attention?"

"You're thinking they were brought in from the other end?" Harold asked thoughtfully.

"It's possible, isn't it? It would have been a lot less obvious."

"True. But the dating is probably important. Before 1776, probably not possible. After? Slightly more likely. I can't date them without examining them more closely because cannon design didn't change very quickly, so the basic model could still have been used in the Civil War. And these are in good shape."

"Does that mean they *weren't* used?" I asked.

"Maybe. Or maybe somebody in 1957 made a Civil War movie here and didn't want to store them afterward. Sorry—the bodies we found would argue against that."

"Hey, Detective?" one of the police called out. "You want us to haul the rest of these out?"

Harold, Marty, Dylan and I looked at each other. "The rest?"

We surged back to the entrance of what I really wanted to call a tunnel—I was already envisioning Society publications describing its intrepid president discovering unknown treasures of Philadelphia— and peered in again. "How many more are there?"

"A coupla dozen, looks like. They go back for a ways."

Harold was now looking like a kid in front of a Christmas tree. "Detective, if you need someplace to store these, I'm sure we can find room at our museum."

She cocked an eyebrow at him. "You really think these are antiques?"

"I think I can prove it. May I?" he asked, advancing on the nearest cannon.

"Go for it," she told him.

With a respectful hand Harold brushed away damp dirt. The brass beneath gleamed dully, and it was easy to imagine what the whole thing would look like if it was cleaned up. It was a handsome piece of metalwork, whatever its age.

"Do you see this here?" Harold asked the group as he gestured toward something on the top surface of the nearest cannon.

"You mean the curly thing with the . . . the thing with the crown on top?" I asked.

"Yes, and those are initials just beneath it. Which are . . ."

It was a lightbulb moment for me when I realized what he was trying to tell us. "G. R. —King George, or George Rex. So you're telling me these date to the Revolution, more or less? They're not pretty reproductions?"

"I'd have to do some more research, but it's certainly possible."

"And the two dead men come from the same era?"

"Maybe," Harold said. "They were more or less on top of the nearer cannons, but they could have been dumped there at the same time, or a century later. Except for that button I found, which would favor the earlier dating."

"And nobody knows who these people were, or why they were here, and where the cannons came from, and how they ended up roughly in the same place and then were completely forgotten, just like the cemetery?"

"I doubt that this was a proper burial. It may be that no one knew they were there. Or that someone knew but didn't want one or the other—or the pair of them—found and so he never told anyone else. Clearly nobody's taken care of this building. Isn't it interesting how structures can simply be abandoned in a major city?"

"There are quite a few examples in some parts of the city," I informed him. "Marty's looking into the details for this block." Although Harold should know about them if he was a proper historian. "So, what do we do now?" I asked nobody in particular.

After an awkward silence, Detective Hrivnak answered my question. "Uh, we don't really know."

"What does that mean?" I asked her.

"Well, the bodies in the onetime cemetery probably belong in some way to whatever church it was—you said you had information on that?" I nodded. "But who is responsible for them now is not clear. The medical examiner is hardly in a position to take them all on, and where does he put them? Is it legal to cremate all those hundreds of remains? Does the city need permission from someone? Is somebody else responsible for them, like a church organization, since the original church doesn't seem to exist anymore? Who decides?"

I smiled ruefully at her. "That is a question that does not usually arise at a library. I assume you'll want to get them off this site as soon as possible?"

"If the archeology types won't make a fuss."

"If they do, I can understand why," I told her. It was true: how often did you get the opportunity to explore this kind of find, a perfect slice of a century of Philadelphia's dead? "So you don't have enough storage, I'm guessing. Harold, what about your museum?"

"Much as I'd love to help out, four hundred-plus bodies is a lot to accommodate, especially if they have to be treated carefully. The cannons are another thing altogether—those we would find room for."

I turned to Barney. "You know of any safe space big enough for all of this? Like an unused warehouse that can be locked?" I figured Barney would have a personal interest in clearing the property so that he could get his crew back to work. Assuming the place wasn't overrun by eager archeologists.

"Maybe," he said dubiously. "Let me check around. Detective, you want it, like, yesterday?"

"More or less," Hrivnak said.

Marty finally spoke. "I can get in touch with the academic community, see if there's any group that would like to help clear these out. You can't just stuff everything in garbage bags and toss them in the back of a truck."

"I'm pretty sure you're right about that," Hrivnak answered. "Sounds like we all have some phone calls to make ASAP. I've got to get back to HQ and get started. I'll leave some officers to guard the place. You all are welcome to stay, as long as you don't walk out with anything."

I had to smile at the image of any of us sauntering away from the site with a cannon tucked under one arm. You'd definitely need a truck to haul even one away.

The detective turned and walked briskly uptown. Harold couldn't take his eyes off the cannons; he was almost drooling. Barney looked . . . bewildered, frustrated, annoyed, excited, take your pick. Here he'd started a nice project in a good neighborhood, and the whole thing had blown up in his face. And a long delay would no doubt cost him money.

I wanted to go back to the Society and pick up where we'd left off, starting with writing a brief report about the original church and cemetery. I hoped it might prod loose some other details. "Have you all had enough for one day, or do you want to get back to researching all this?" I asked the small group.

Dylan volunteered, "I'm still working on the genealogy side. Maybe I'm not the best person to be handling that, since I don't have a lot of experience, but I can probably figure out who lived in this building or along the street, with Marty's help, and maybe why the cannons were hidden here."

"You need to have a date first," Harold pointed out quickly.

"So which comes first?" Dylan replied. "We know the bodies are old, because of that button you pulled off one. Unless that guy was a fancy reenactor, which doesn't seem likely. The two bodies were found sort of in front of and on top of the cannons, so it sounds like they went into the hole at the same time or after the cannons did. The cannons look old, but how do you tell? Harold, you're the expert."

"A number of ways. The composition of the metal. Whether there are any comparable examples known, and how well they match, in terms of design and size. Whether those there were found around Philadelphia or somewhere else."

"Like in England somewhere?" Dylan seemed to be getting into the idea.

"Maybe," Harold said. "But we can't just assume that the bodies and the cannons come from the same era. Or even that the two bodies match in time."

I was getting hungry again, and we'd spent the entire afternoon watching people haul possibly antique cannons through the dirt. "Look, people, for the moment we're the only ones who know about all this and are researching it. I can't imagine the police department will want this to drag on. We need to come up with some answers quickly—but not by taking shortcuts. I suggest that we all pursue our own paths, like we've been doing, and then we can get together and compare notes. How much time will it take?"

Harold snorted. "As long as it takes. These artifacts may be well over two hundred years old, or they may be much less—it's going to take time to narrow things down. Can we meet tomorrow?"

Tomorrow being Tuesday, the Society would be open to the public. While that didn't directly affect me, it might get in Dylan's way, and Marty's if she chose to work at the Society rather than at home. And I was beginning to wonder if I'd ever finish the board report. I really needed to come up with a spectacular find to justify dragging my heels on the financial statements. "Fine with me. You all want to meet at the Society tomorrow morning?"

"What about the museum?" Harold protested. "There might be other things worth looking at, as a basis for comparison to these cannons."

"True. How about this? We start out at the Society and then walk over to your place, and you can show us any comparables that are relevant?"

"I guess that would do," he said reluctantly. "Ten o'clock?"

"Does that work for everyone?" Everyone nodded. "Then I'm going home now, but I'll be back early tomorrow. And I'm guessing we're all going to keep working on this tonight, so we'll have more information to work with in the morning. Good night, all."

I left the former cemetery site after waving goodbye to everyone. I walked about a block away and found a bench and sat, and called James.

"You're still at work?" I asked when he picked up.

"Thinking about leaving. You?"

"I'm on a bench near Independence Hall. It's been a busy day. Can you leave now?"

"I don't see why not. I'll meet you downstairs in ten."

Chapter Seventeen

I arrived in front of James's building just as he was emerging from the main entrance. "You look tired," was his first comment.

"That's because I am tired. But it's been an interesting day, to say the least."

"Let's get the car and head home—you can tell me all about it on the way."

I stayed quiet while he maneuvered his way out of the parking lot and headed for the suburbs. Once he was headed north, out of city traffic, I felt free to talk. "I feel like each of us is trying to research and produce a thesis in only two or three days. At least there are three of us—no, four—looking at different aspects."

"You're still talking about the lost cemetery?"

"That's only one part of it. After hearing Marty's story, the police took a harder look at that first body. Only it turned out to be two bodies, more or less tangled together, and behind them were pristine British cannons with King George's initials on them."

"Which means they date from the Revolution?"

"Maybe. But right now we have no guesses as to why they are there and who the dead men are and why the dead men were more or less lying on the cannons. In the meantime, the police department is trying to figure out where to put four hundred other dead bodies."

"The cemetery?"

"Yup. Wonder of wonders, the Society actually has a print copy of those people who were buried there, but there's no guarantee that it's a complete list, or who got moved to the other cemetery. I have a gut feeling that there was some skulduggery there in the nineteenth century, but I really don't have time to explore all the options. Suffice it to say, I think the church people just got tired of moving bodies, or ran out of money, and quietly covered them over. Is that a crime?"

James answered seriously. "I have no clue as to who owns dead bodies, here or elsewhere, or who was responsible for their ultimate disposition. But I'm pretty sure that now that they've been revealed, the city can't just cover them up again. Should be interesting to see if they can find a law that covers that."

He drove in silence for another mile or two. "So, you said there are four people working on this now?"

"Yes—Harold Stevens, another contact of Marty's. She seems to know everyone in the city. He's the expert on artillery at the new Revolutionary War museum, and we thought we should have someone with some experience look at the cannons. He was very excited."

"Don't they already have cannons at his place?" James asked.

"Sure, but just a few. They don't have a couple of dozen."

"What?"

"Yes, a whole batch of matching, never-used large bronze cannons with King George's initials on them."

"I would call that a 'find' by any standards. What are you going to do about them?"

"Detective Hrivnak is letting us look into all the details, as long as we can do it fast. She doesn't want to leave a large pit full of bones open in the tourist part of the city, which I can understand. But then there's the problem of what to do with all the bodies. And I fully expect the archeological slash historical community, academic or other, to descend like a flock of vultures looking for details."

"And you want to get ahead of them?"

"Only for the first announcement. None of us—at least, not Marty and me—are experts, although Harold is, and Dylan's working on it—but Marty and I want bragging rights for the discovery, to promote the Society. I know, that sounds self-serving, but our discovery could be important, and it's certainly interesting. And in my personal opinion, it seems almost criminal to simply put all that evidence of Philadelphia's past in boxes and file it in some basement somewhere. I know I already feel different about that neighborhood, and I've been working in that part of town and, heck, even walking by all those bodies without even knowing it. I feel like I have an obligation to figure out what went wrong there, as a public member of the museum community."

"I can respect that. But I do have to wonder if you've been hanging out with me too much. You're treating this as a forensic exercise—here is the victim, cause of death was whatever, weapon was something-or-other, and then you start looking at identifying the victims, and finding out if they were local or from somewhere else, if they knew each other, or if other people in the city knew them. And so on. Maybe there's a series in it for you."

"You mean broadcast? Could be fun, but we can't count on finding a new body a week. At least, I hope not. You want to help? You find the bodies, and I and my fearless and overeducated team solves the crime, assuming there was one."

"I'd have to clear it with the FBI. Is there a crime here?"

"For Marty's two men, I'm pretty sure there was, although the medical examiner is going to have something to say about that. We did ask that he examine those two bodies first, to determine cause of death. There was nothing obvious, but it was hard to see much. If we do find projectiles, I guess Harold would be the best person to ask. As for the cemetery issue, I think that's more a legal issue, since everybody who was found there was dead when they were placed there. Since I've already figured out what church was originally involved, and what happened through the years, I'm less concerned about that. Although maybe someone in the Philadelphia medical community would be interested in examining the corpses to see how they died. Once we assign them dates, of course, and that spans well over a hundred years. That's one place the Society published list could come in handy."

James was smiling, and I realized he had been for a while. "Have you listened to yourself? Did you ever think that you, as a professional fund-raiser and library administrator with an English degree, would be taking the lead in investigating a crime or crimes that happened a couple of hundred years ago?"

"Should I apply to the FBI for a job? You know, my research indicates that there are probably a lot of forgotten cemeteries in the city—maybe I should specialize in identifying old anonymous corpses."

"You're enjoying this," James stated. It was not a question.

"You know, I am. But it isn't as crazy as it sounds. The Society is keeper of much of the written history of the city, and we're always looking for more. Why bother to collect all this stuff if not to put it to practical use? I don't mean specifically hunting for bodies, but why are some buildings where they are? Why are some preserved and others torn down to make way for parking lots? And it doesn't all have to be about the really old stuff. How many people know who John Wanamaker was? Why was the Reading Terminal Market preserved while any connections to the Reading Railroad are long gone? I'll admit it: this kind of stuff fascinates me. We need to know at least some of our own history."

"You don't have to convince me, Nell. I agree," James said quietly.

"Good. Now can we think about dinner?"

Once back home, fussing over pots and pans (easy spaghetti: boil water, cook pasta, open a jar of sauce, dump some grated cheese on it—and pour a couple of glasses of wine to go with it), I found I couldn't turn off my brain. Yes, I was having fun solving a puzzle, albeit one with a lot of pieces missing. Yes, I was enjoying working with other like-minded people and pooling what information we found. And yes, I could see a way that this could benefit the Society, which was paying my salary. And I enjoyed laying hands on antique items, not because they were valuable but before they themselves had a long history. Maybe I always hoped for a glimmer of a psychic connection to a book or somebody's silver teaspoon. It hadn't happened yet, but I kept hoping. Of course, I'd never tried it on a humongous cannon—

maybe that would have held on to more psychic vibrations over time. Unless of course all of them were fake. Heck, maybe they'd been created solely to muddy the deaths of the two men. So one had a nice old button—there were plenty of those available online for a small fee. If I was going to camouflage a recent death or two by making it look like a long-ago death, how would I go about it?

"Nell?"

"Huh? Or, what?"

"Are you going to sleep?" James asked.

"Maybe. Shoot, we're supposed to meet at the Society in the morning. Are you planning to drive?"

"I am. You need a ride?"

"Yes, please."

We cleaned up the kitchen (one pot, two plates) and went to bed early, and then awoke early. I hadn't changed my mind overnight: I was still enjoying the effort of trying to understand why all those bodies had emerged only this past week, after lying in (or on) the ground for a century or two. It didn't seem logical, but there had to be a reason. And my band of friends and colleagues, coupled with the resources of our combined institutions (as well as Marty's family library) gave us material that might help us find answers. I guess I had forgotten that history could be fun, not something boring from a book that had to be memorized for a test at school. And we were living (Marty) and working (me) in the midst of all that history, even though most people couldn't see it as they trudged by. There had to be a way to make history more vivid to people.

Chapter Eighteen

When I was getting ready for work, I realized I had a full day's work ahead of me plus a meeting with Harold, Marty and Dylan about the cemetery and the two dead men with the cannons. That was easily two days of work, and my heart was racing even before I stepped out of the shower.

After a hurried breakfast, James and I took off for Center City. I was glad he'd volunteered to drive. Much as I enjoyed taking the train, it was sometimes unpredictable, and I needed all the time I could scrounge if I hoped to finish anything today.

When James dropped me off in front of the Society building it wasn't even nine o'clock, but our little band of researchers was already waiting, sitting on the top steps in front. For a moment I thought it was funny that we were all so excited about investigating dead people, but I'd long since learned that historians had unusual tastes. Besides, these particular dead people had a place in the city's history, if only we could figure out what it was.

I got out of the car and greeted them. "You're early, but then, so am I. Let's meet in the conference room under the stairs, and then we can take off for Harold's place. Assuming you don't have a mountain of materials to spread out. I apologize in advance that I haven't had time to add anything new since yesterday to the information we've collected, unless you count how to share this with the public most effectively. Which is, after all, my job."

"Nell, let's just go in now, shall we?" Marty said. She sounded grumpy.

"Okay, okay," I muttered. I unlocked the door and we trooped in, turning left in the lobby to reach the original conference room that was concealed under the grand staircase and was seldom used now. We settled around the long table and spread out what notes we'd brought.

"If I may make a comment," I began, "I say we should start with the two dead men and the cannons. The cemetery bodies are more appropriately the city's jurisdiction, and while we can answer some basic questions like what church they were associated with, and maybe what went wrong, it's beyond our scope. I have a feeling that the two men under the house fall more in our jurisdiction. There may be some overlap, but I think we need to focus. Agreed?"

Everyone nodded solemnly.

I turned to Harold. "Harold, am I right in thinking that we need to look at the cannons first and the bodies second? It's quite possible they're connected, but authenticating and dating the cannons should give us some insight into the bodies."

"I think you're right," Harold said. "As you might guess, I went back to the museum after we parted last night and examined those pieces most like the ones we've found, as well as their condition. I'd be happy to share with you the entire history of cannon manufacture, but I suppose we should save that for another time, so I'll give you the short form. Artillery was manufactured in multiple places, but we are most concerned with England and this country. Cannons in a variety of sizes and configurations were the mainstay of battles on this continent in the seventeenth century and beyond. The forges were most often located as close as possible to the raw materials, such as coal, which would be necessary to melt the metal for casting. Pennsylvania had an ample supply of those materials. And as you might also guess, there was a need for materials for the carriages to move the cannons themselves. You can't just drag a cannon to the battlefield, so you need something with wheels. And don't forget the ammunition and the gunpowder necessary to fire them. Of course, when managed correctly, they have an amazing range—as much as a mile or more."

I felt I had to interrupt him. "Harold, you are a font of information and I'd love to know more, but can we get to the point? We can look up the history of cannons on our own."

Harold sighed. "I do get rather enthusiastic. But to cut to the chase, in my opinion those cannons that emerged yesterday are authentic, were made in England and shipped to Philadelphia in a single shipment, but were never fired. And they most likely date to the 1770s, based on my comparisons with similar weapons."

"One shipment?" Dylan asked.

"Yes. They are all in the same condition, and also share some distinctive casting marks."

"So we can reasonably guess that they were shipped here to support the British war effort?" I asked.

"That would be likely," Harold said.

"So how did they end up under a house here? Admittedly it was near the river, so can we assume they were delivered to Philadelphia by boat?"

"I would say so."

"Why did they not end up where they belonged?" I asked.

"That is harder to answer," Harold admitted. "You have seen that at least one of the two dead men may have been British, based on the rather slim evidence of the button. But he alone, or even with the help of a second man, could not have easily transported one cannon of that size, much less two dozen of them. Certainly not through one of the busiest parts of the city. There had to have been others involved."

"And why choose that spot?" I pressed on. "Sure, it was close to the river, which would have made it relatively easier to unload them. With help, anyway. But why that particular house? From what little we've looked at, there were quite a few vacant properties in that area that would have served. Stuffing them all under a residential house, rather than, say, a warehouse or a boatyard, was not an obvious choice. At the very least it doesn't seem well-planned. I could understand moving around boxes of muskets, but cannons?"

"Maybe it was a spur-of-the-moment decision?" Marty suggested. She'd been suspiciously quiet, not just this morning but for the last few days. Had she been that rattled by finding the body from her childhood? And she hadn't even known about the second one. Or did she have some inkling of an explanation but wasn't ready to share it? She knew more about the nuts and bolts of Old Philadelphia than anyone else I knew. Why should she hide information?

Harold seemed to snap to attention once again. "So, let us assume we now have a date—the 1770s—and a reason for them to be here— the fledgling American Revolution. Which leaves us with some rather important questions. One, how did they get here? Two, why were they never used, by either side, in the conflict? Three, who was responsible for that oversight?"

I volunteered, "I'll be the first to admit that I don't know a lot about that era—or maybe era is stretching it. That early time of the Revolution must have been chaotic in this city. Nobody was quite sure who to trust, or which way they leaned politically. A lot of people who could afford it left the city for the country, thinking it might be safer. But daily life went on. You have only to look at old city maps of the waterfront to see how much shipping and presumably shipbuilding was going on then. And as it applies to our problem here, all those changes meant that even if there had been a 1770 or 1780 census, many houses might have been empty at the time."

"There are earlier lists—tax records and such," Harold said, his tone contemptuous.

"Harold, I know that, at least in general terms. But will that point us to a particular person or building?"

He sighed. "Does it really matter?"

That surprised me. "You don't think so? Aren't you curious? We're talking about an important time in both national and local history. Somebody had a stash of high-end weapons and sat on them, possibly through the war. Don't you want to know who and why? There may be other legal and practical issues beyond that, like who do the cannons belong to now? The city? Can they be auctioned?

Would your museum like some or all of them? And who would benefit?"

Harold looked only slightly mollified. "Nell, I've had all of one day to process their existence. I can't answer questions like that now. And you're looking for a story, not simple facts. I'll admit there could be some drama involved, but I'm not ready to address that."

"Okay, I understand. Will you be annoyed if the rest of us pursue the drama part? I don't think any of us can afford to put a lot of time into searching, but we still haven't fully explored who owned or occupied which house, which in turn could lead to how the cannons came to be there, and who the bodies are. I think the city is obligated to make an effort to identify the dead, and we can help with that."

"I suppose," Harold said without much enthusiasm. "Are we ready to go over to the museum now?"

I was annoyed at him, but clearly he had no interest in the people involved with the cannons. Marty, Dylan and I could handle the people on our own. "We can do that, then Marty and Dylan can come back here with me. Okay?" Both Dylan and Marty nodded enthusiastically—I think Harold was getting on everyone's nerves, but at least he'd given us the information we needed: the cannons were genuine and dated to the 1770s. Now we had to go collect all the rest of the facts.

I would have enjoyed the behind-the-scenes tour of the new museum, which I'd barely skimmed on my only visit, if I had not been trying to work out the whos and whys of the cannons. That they were in some way part of the Revolutionary War effort seemed an obvious guess, but why had they never been put to use? An awful lot of things seemed to have been forgotten in that single block—a crowd of hundreds of burials from a church that no longer existed, and a couple of dozen pristine military weapons and the two bodies that had guarded them in death. But for which side? And apart from the dead men, had no one in the city or either army known that they were there or even that they had existed? It didn't quite make sense. I had the odd feeling that either we'd find the answer quickly or not at all. After all, how many people kept good records of such a troubled and rapidly changing time, and even if they had, how many of those records had survived? Much less to the level of detail to pinpoint that very specific location.

We stayed at Harold's museum long enough to be polite, but left as soon as we could: we still had work to do at the Society. As we walked two blocks back, I resumed my role as leader. "All right, troops, we now have a fairly clear date for the cache, around 1775. Of course at that time a year in either direction would make a big difference. We can also assume that the two bodies are from the same era as the cannons, and they may well have died in a single encounter. Don't protest—I'm making this up as I go, but what I've suggested is at least possible. Where do we go from here? Marty?"

"I'm still working on a definitive list of who lived in the block of houses, or if the houses were vacant, who owned them at that time. We've already found a bookbinder, but he was active a bit later than our focus, so if anything, he would have been preserving a history of recent events, given the map. Dylan, please keep an eye out for any other insertions—maybe there's more." She paused for a moment. "We haven't discussed the likelihood that the cannons were removed from a ship tied up at a dock on the Delaware River. I mean to ask Harold about it, but I wanted to hang on to some control of this search, and he's a bit too eager for my taste. But if it was a ship, did it run aground? Was it captured and the contents seized? By which side? And what ship?"

I almost smiled. "Marty, I know the bare minimum about things military in that war, and even less about ships. Feel free to investigate. Dylan, I've given you a double load. I asked you to review all of Harriet's collection and put it in some sort of order, and I also asked that you sketch out a basic family tree for her. Did she always live in Philadelphia? And she never married, so we know her surname, but not much more than that."

"I can help Dylan with that, at least for the last century or so," Marty volunteered. "That is, if you don't mind me butting in, Dylan."

"I'd really appreciate your help, Ms. Terwilliger," he said. He sounded like he meant it. He sure was getting a learning experience out of this internship.

"Perfect. I can put together a summary of what we know, at least by the end of today, and present it to Detective Hrivnak, and maybe the medical examiner. It might make their lives easier. Do you think we can finish the basic outline by the end of today? That would keep us in the police's good graces, and would give us a basic structure for any publicity we get a chance to offer."

"Works for me," Marty said. "Dylan, you in?"

"Sure. This really is great stuff. Thanks for including me."

. "So, we all have our marching orders. Can we meet before opening time tomorrow for a quick once-over of what we've got?"

Nods all around.

Dylan was right: this was fun. Of course it was sad that there were so many bodies involved, and that for the two dead men and the cannons, whatever happened had taken place during the early stages of a war. But solving the puzzle—especially one set in the real world, if long ago—was a great and important challenge. "Then let's get started!"

We parted in different directions to pursue our assigned tasks.

I lost track of time—which often happened to me when I was digging into interesting research—so was surprised when my phone vibrated. It was James—I'd forgotten he was going to give me a ride home. I didn't see any point to letting Dylan and Marty know I was leaving, since we'd already made out plans for the next day, so I went downstairs to meet him.

"How's your search going?" James said, although he sounded distracted—traffic was heavier than usual for some reason.

"Good. Harold gave us some solid information. We now believe that the two mystery bodies do date from the eighteenth century, and at least one of them was English. And the cannons are authentic: made in England under King George, all matching, and never fired. Harold was quite excited. However, we have not determined how they ended up under that house and who put them there."

"So what's your next step?"

"Marty is looking at property and tax records, censuses and whatever lists of names existed for the later eighteenth century in that neighborhood, which was already pretty well populated at that time. If she can't find a name to put to the house, nobody in the city can."

"Agreed. But does it matter?"

I turned to face him. "Of course it does. They are British-made cannons hidden on American soil, at a date that strongly suggests the start of the Revolutionary War. So whose they were is important. And so was who hid them. Which side? If I remember my history correctly, the years around 1775 were pivotal to the war effort. Were the cannons intended to be used in battle, or did someone acquire them and hide them so they *wouldn't* be used in battle? Kept hidden from whichever the perpetrator considered the 'wrong' side?"

"Interesting," James commented. "So how does Marty plan to figure this out?"

"Because she knows who was who in that part of town back then, and because she had ancestors there and has spent a large part of her life researching them and their families and friends. She would know who officially supported which side, and who might have concealed his true allegiance. Or say the house was vacant because the owners or residents—not always the same thing—had packed up and left town until things cooled down. Which might not help our case, but I refuse to believe that a group of people—and it would have taken a group, given the weight of even a single cannon—was running around in the dark moving them to hide them and nobody noticed. There must be some kind of record somewhere."

"Fair enough. What's next?"

"Marty will present what she's found to us tomorrow, I hope.

Dylan is wrapping up looking at the rest of Harriet Featherstone's donation, for both physical condition and content. And, I suppose, if there's anything else hidden somewhere in the collection. And I'm supposed to pull it all together and give the basic outline to Detective Hrivnak, which should give us some credit with the police department, and work on the board presentation and budget for the coming meeting. Maybe I can shift the emphasis just a bit, if it looks like there's a good story with all these bodies, or just the ones with the cannons. And the Society did find the original document, and more, so I think we should get first rights."

"You sound really enthusiastic," James commented.

"I am. For one thing, this all has made me realize I've lost sight of the history of what was happening in Philadelphia back then, while I concentrated on the financial side of my job. I think I need to find a better balance, and this is a great opportunity. And beyond that, finding the two bodies and the cannons makes history more real, to me and hopefully to other people. The thing is, we still need to figure out who was who, if it's even possible. Harold thinks one of the men was English, but was he the one who hid the cannons? We don't know about the other man—there's not a lot left of him or his clothes to work with. Were the two men on the same side, guarding the weapons until what most people would have guessed was the coming battle? Or were they on opposite sides, and both died fighting each other for control? Maybe there's something in our records about captured ships—although I guess if our side had seized a ship with that cargo, they wouldn't have told the world, or at least not until after the battle. Yes, before you remind me, I need to learn more about the Battle of Trenton—how that came about, and what armaments the two sides were fighting with. Anyway, however this all works out, it's a pretty safe guess that the cannons were hidden at a pivotal point in the American Revolution, and I want to know more. Does that make sense?"

"It does. You really seen caught up in it."

"I guess I am. Not because I have a ghoulish affection for long-dead bodies, but because we're here where it all happened. It's too easy to lose sight of that, and yet a lot of the history is still right there under our feet. I work for a renowned historical institution in one of the first major cities of this country, and there's too much that I don't know. And I'm supposed to be convincing donors to give me —or the Society—money to support us. I don't think I've been doing as effective a job as I could be, and here is the perfect opportunity to do something about it," I said firmly. "So, yes, I'm excited that I can make a difference. Is that enough?"

"Yes, thank you very much. I know far less than you do. And I agree that we should humanize history, for visitors and for schools, and hope that they remember some of what they learn."

"Good. At least we'll have something to talk about over dinner," I told him, smiling. "So, to get back to your original questions, I've got the church records in hand, and the reports of what the church *said* they were doing with the bodies. I'm sure Marty will have a summary ready by tomorrow—she's already got a head start, and it's not a very large area. I wish we could ask Harold about any British boats that were captured, but he seems a little too eager to involve himself in this search. I'm willing to admit he is best suited to handle this, and maybe in the long run his museum will end up with the cannons, or at least some of them, but as I said, I'm staking my claim first. And who knows what Dylan may find? He's young and inexperienced, but he has sharp eyes and a different perspective, so I'm hoping he comes up with something good. You have anything to add? By the way, thanks for letting us borrow your lab for the ink analysis—that's what got us started in the right direction."

"Happy to be of service to you, ma'am. And to your library, and to the City of Philadelphia, and the history of the United States. Besides, it's more interesting than the stack of reports on my desk."

"Well, I guess that's something," I said, and fell silent for the rest of the ride home.

Chapter Nineteen

Dylan had left on my desk after I'd gone a tidy summary of his research to date. To me it seemed unlikely that Dylan had found the key to something or other by doing exactly what I had asked him to. But his instincts had been right when he found the original map in the book, and then brought it to Marty and me and started this whole thing rolling. Was it really less than a week ago? I trusted him enough to know that I had to look at what he'd just found, but it was unrealistic to expect that there would be a single tidy explanation of everything that had happened since 1775 up until last Thursday. *Read it already, Nell!* I told myself, and sought out a quiet corner with a semi-comfortable chair.

It looked to me as though Dylan had done only rudimentary genealogy until now, but his results were clear enough. Typically, he had started with Harriet and worked backward. I had to force myself not to look at the early years immediately: I too would start with Harriet and work my way up the line, noting any details that needed to be verified. At least I had known Harriet, if only slightly—Marty would have known her better. In my memory she was a short cheerful woman of advanced years. She was also the only person I had ever known about whom I would say "her eyes twinkled."

Apparently she'd never married, nor had any children. If Dylan had got the tree right, she'd outlived her parents for a good many years. They too had been Philadelphia city dwellers for all their lives, and their parents before them (I struggled to restrain myself from checking each generation immediately—besides, given Dylan's enthusiasm, I inferred that he had made sure that the family had most likely been Philadelphians for a long time).

Since Harriet had remained unmarried, the Featherstone surname continued back to the earliest names Dylan had included. That made things a bit easier to follow. The earliest family birth date Dylan had included was 1748. After I'd followed the tree to its conclusion, I took a deep breath and picked up a copy of the 1790 census, and looked for Featherstone on Arch Street. And found it, attached to a street number that I recognized. We had our house's occupant, and very likely one of the men buried with the cannons. But which one?

Dylan rapped softly on the door frame of the room where I'd hidden myself away. "You finished reading yet?"

"Not quite. I've just gotten to the Arch Street Featherstone family. How much more is there?"

"Maybe ten pages. The last part is a letter that Harriet wrote—it was inside a book, but not bound into it. I put a copy in your folder. And I gave a copy to Marty too, before she left last night. Do you want me to tell you what I think it means, or would you rather read it first?"

"Give me a few minutes to read, and then we can compare notes. You don't have to leave—I read fast. If I didn't, I wouldn't have survived here very long."

Dylan smiled. "I hear you. I'll wait."

I smiled briefly at him and then dug into the final piece. Thank goodness it was a relatively modern piece of paper, or it would have been illegible, although it appeared that Harriett had written it a good number of years earlier.

It began:

> My name is Harriet Featherstone, and I live in Philadelphia. So did most of my ancestors. If you're reading this, it means that I've passed on and left my collection of books to the Society. The books are a real hodgepodge, because I collected books that interested me, regardless of subject, age or financial value. But this letter is my own addition. It is about a particular episode of my family's history in the city. To the best of my knowledge, the information contained in this letter was never published or shared. As I know my time is

short, I believe that this incident should be recorded, but if it is never found I will not be troubled. I'll leave it in the hands of fate.

My most distant Featherstone ancestor, Samuel, arrived in Philadelphia by ship in 1743 and quickly found work on the docks. He raised his family near the river, and I am descended from his eldest son, Josiah. His father died in the 1770s, a time of turmoil in Philadelphia and beyond. It is his story I wish to share.

I had a feeling I knew what was coming, but as it turned out I was only partly right. I read Harriet's letter through, then went back and checked a few details to be sure I'd understood them correctly. Then I returned it to its folder and looked at Dylan. "Well, that was unexpected."

Dylan nodded. "Did you know Harriet Featherstone?"

"Only in passing, at events here. She was a nice lady—she loved doing research, so sometimes we'd talk about what she was working on. But somehow we never quite got around to talking about her family. I have to wonder what Marty has made of this letter. She's the one with deep roots here."

I sat back in my chair. "So let me run through the facts as I understand them. Harriet's earliest American ancestor came to Philadelphia and settled in that house on Arch Street—there was a Featherstone there in the 1790 census." Dylan nodded in agreement. "He worked in the shipyards, so he knew ships—and probably knew ship traffic in the 1770s. He could well have heard somehow of the expected shipment of British cannons. Now, the question becomes, which side was he on? When I was reading the letter, I came up with two guesses: either he was a Loyalist and was holding the guns until the British could claim them, or he was a Patriot and fought with whichever British soldier or ship's captain found out where they were hidden, and they both ended up dead. Which way did you interpret it?" I asked Dylan, and waited curiously for his response.

"The second one, I think. Not because we have any evidence as such, but because Harriett seemed to be ashamed of whatever had happened and she hesitated before recording it. I'm guessing it was because her great-great-whatever had killed a man, but it might have been because she felt he had fought for the wrong side. She was very careful about how she phrased things. Sad that even now it troubled her."

"Ashamed of being descended from a Loyalist or British soldier, or of being descended from a killer? Which do you think she would have seen as the worse?"

"Could go either way, but I'd go with the Loyalist. You said she enjoyed looking into family history. This letter here isn't new, so she must have found this information quite a while ago, and it hadn't discouraged her from recording it. As for feeling regret for how the soldier died—well, it was more or less wartime, and from what little I know of the woman, based mainly on the books she collected, she was an ardent Patriot and proud of that heritage. I'd guess she'd hoped the killing never came out, but she wasn't going to alter the story just because it bothered her. And the man had died for his sins, which might have mitigated his act. She was an honest person."

"Dylan, I hope you're right. Let's let Marty make the final call— she knows more about this kind of thing than the two of us put together."

Marty chose that moment to make her appearance. "You've read it, right?"

"We have. We still have two dead men, but who died first, and at whose hand? Your guess?"

"I say Featherstone killed a soldier—the one with the button. I told you, I knew Harriet's mother. She was very proud of her heritage, and she passed that on to Harriet. We know that soldiers in war kill others, but she would have to have believed that the death was justified. Otherwise she might have stopped talking about it."

"Makes sense, sort of," I said. "Can you put a name to Button Man?"

"Not yet. Maybe never. I'll keep looking."

"Have we found any record of a missing shipment of cannons?" I asked.

"No, but that doesn't mean there isn't a record. Anyway, those times were kind of chaotic, so that may not be easy to find. If it even exists. There were various independent ship's captains who managed to commandeer British vessels coming up the Delaware River, and you can imagine how reluctant both sides would have been to record events like that or make them public. I'm willing to guess that's the source of those cannons, but I'll keep looking at ships records for that time."

Marty dropped into a chair, and we all sat in silence for a few moments, fitting the pieces together mentally. Two men had died, one from each side of a major conflict that had barely started. The shipment of cannons had lain, forgotten, under a decrepit house for over two centuries. The two men who had died had probably been the only two who knew where the cannons were stashed, and they took their secret with them when they died, and then they had been forgotten too, except by Harriet Featherstone's family. Who had left a map and the letter before us.

"What do we do now?" I said softly, almost to myself.

"No need to hurry," Marty said. "It's been a secret this long—what's a little more time?"

"But who *should* know?" I demanded.

"It depends. Yeah, I know that's no help. What we've got right now is a big cemetery that was completely forgotten. And that's bound to make headlines when the word gets out—and there's no way to hide the site. The police and the city are wrestling with what to do about that whole mess, and I don't envy them. Then there's the abandoned house and two bodies and a stack of eighteenth-century cannons. The police know about the bodies—I think they have to report all bodies—but the cemetery bodies outrank those other two right now. The police may just lump our two into that huge number and not worry about investigating. Now, we—you, Dylan and me—have a choice about how to present what we've found to the police, or even the news media. Since we don't want to make the police look foolish, we should probably be careful and write up what we found separately, so it doesn't look like they missed something obvious. You can talk to your detective personally when you hand her our findings."

"My detective?"

"You know her better than the rest of us."

"I guess. But our list isn't complete. James knows, obviously, though I'm sure he hasn't shared it. Barney, although he didn't know anything about the Second Street bodies until we told him. Harold, because we told him about them and asked for his help with dating both the bodies and the cannons."

"True," Marty acknowledged. "This is beginning to sound like a press conference. Or two."

"And we'd better do it fast, before someone scoops us. The original discovery belongs to the Society. What do you think should happen with the cannons?"

"I'd leave that with Harold—he's the expert. But we do want to keep the Society front and center in whatever news goes out, for promotional reasons."

"Now what?" Dylan asked. I wished I had a better option for him.

"I will type up a brief summary of what we know—the identity of the big cemetery, what little we know about the identity of the two men with the cannons, our guesses about where the cannons came from, and maybe a short list of what could be done with them now. It won't be detailed, but at least it will stake our claim to part of it. Is that okay with you?"

Marty answered quickly. "There's a lot more that can be done in the way of research, but I agree that we should make it public, in case anything goes wrong. And it gives us the opportunity to control at least a small part of the outcome."

"You going to talk to Harold?" I asked her.

"I think I'll wait until you and the detective work out whatever your deal will be. And don't forget to get her permission to talk with the press. Or go together to do it."

"Yes, ma'am!"

Finally we had a plan. Marty and Dylan disappeared into the stacks to look for more facts, and I headed for my computer to draft a quick but catchy summary of what we'd found in the past few days.

Chapter Twenty

I decided before I started composing a short, pithy, persuasive summary of what Marty, Dylan and I had put together that I ought to call Detective Hrivnak and make sure that she was in her office or nearby, and that she might actually want to hear what we now knew. I hadn't seen any major announcement in the news about the bodies from the lost cemetery or our two outliers, so maybe the police department still didn't know what they wanted to say. And I could help them.

I hit speed-dial for her number (ignoring the unlikely fact that I had a police detective programmed into my phone, and had for a while) and was lucky to find her there. Albeit peevish. "What?" she barked.

"This is Nell Pratt. I've got some information on your various dead people, if you're still interested."

"Information like what?"

"Which church managed the cemetery. Names for a lot of the people who were buried there. Where they did or did not end up and why."

"Oh." The detective was silent for a moment. "Can you email it? Fax it?"

"Of course I could, but I'd like a couple of minutes to talk to you first."

"I should have a couple of minutes to spare, oh, next month some-time."

"I'm serious. I won't take long. Tell me, what have you told the press?"

"Nothing yet, because we'd look like idiots. You know, 'we found a couple of hundred bodies in our backyard but we don't know who they are or why they're here.'"

"And I can help you with that," I said firmly. "I'll be there in fifteen minutes." I hung up before she could say no, and turned to my keyboard. *Keep it short and simple,* I told myself—*and include copies of some of the materials in case she wants more details* (which I doubted). It would take me five minutes, max.

In fact it took ten. I debated about bringing Marty and Dylan with me, but I figured even a small crowd would not make the busy detective happy, and I had all the information from them anyway. I messaged Marty and Dylan about where I was going, gathered up my stuff, and made my escape before they could waylay me and want to tag along.

Another nice day. Why, I wondered, did I spend all these lovely summer days inside the Society, or trampling through very old muck sprinkled with even older bodies, or speculating about the age, weight and origin of cannons? I still knew next to nothing about cannons. I knew a bit more about bodies, but all in all, I'd rather know more about cannons. I arrived at the police head-quarters only a few minutes late, and the detective arrived a few minutes later to escort me upstairs. Maybe I should call James about having lunch.

When we reached her floor, she opted to head for the same small interview room we'd used before. She dropped into a chair, and I sat more gently. Poor Detective Hrivnak was looking kind of frazzled, and I hoped my news might make her feel better.

"What've you got?" she demanded without preamble.

"I'll give you the short form—you can ask questions later. I've identified the church that opened the cemetery." I slid my first xerox across the table toward her. "It's no longer there, and the congregation moved several times before it was absorbed by another church, but at least it gives you a name. Next, there was an official notice about moving the cemetery"—I slid another page toward her, a copy of the old newspaper article—"although I don't know if there are any records of how many bodies were transferred to Mount Moriah. That would take a bit more searching. Third, it turns out the Society has a published report on the names of those who were buried in the old cemetery. I don't know if you want to follow up on that, but at least it's available. I can print you out a full copy if you want."

"Is that all?" she asked, but in a slightly softer tone.

"No. I had Martha Terwilliger and Dylan Robertson working with me. We believe we have identified the two other men who were found with the cannons—Harold Stevens helped us with dating the artillery, as well as that one button that was found. One of the men most likely lived in the house where they were found. The other was apparently a British soldier."

I debated briefly with myself about telling her the connection to Harriet, but she'd kept her secret for so long I couldn't bring myself to tell the police about it. But then I changed my mind: Harriet had recognized the event as an important piece of history, and had shared it with the Society. There was no one left in the Featherstone family who could be hurt by the truth, and in fact Harriet's ancestor had done an important service to the country. "We also found a letter written by Harriet Featherstone, who gave us the collection of books that started all this. It wasn't hidden, at least not in the same way as the map, but she didn't exactly want it made public. She wanted the Society to have it because of its historical significance. She said she was descended from the owner of the house, the one who wasn't the British soldier, and she laid out the whole story. Here's a copy of that letter. Dylan worked out the genealogy, and Marty confirmed it. You can read it when you have time."

"So it was murder?" the detective asked.

"Murder if you include that among acts of war. It's possible that the cannons were intended to be turned over to the British forces and would have been used in the Battle of Trenton, as well as other battles, but the Patriots seized them and hid them. Given the weather before the battle, it was unlikely they would have made the river crossing, and the two men who knew what they were and where they were hidden apparently killed each other. They were never used."

"Wow," Detective Hrivnak said. "You put all these pieces together in less than a week?"

"We're historians, Marty and Dylan and me. With some help from Harold Stevens. The information wasn't hard to find, if you knew what you were looking for. So Barney's accidental discovery of all those bodies led to the addition of a small piece of history, for Philadelphia and for the Revolution." We both paused briefly, to give proper consideration to what we had learned. Then I said, "Anything new on your end?"

"Not really. The city is still arguing between departments, trying to decide who's in charge of the cemetery mess. The medical examiner is tearing out his hair. The professor types are calling every couple of hours asking if they can do a formal dig or at least get access to some of the remains. We've been keeping round-the-clock police guards around the site, which is costing us money, and to protect those cannons. Those suckers are heavy!"

"That they are. And they could be worth some good money, if you can figure out who owns them."

"Harold Stevens has been eager to help us, believe me. Does that museum of his need any more cannons?"

"I think they've got that covered, but as I said, they could be valuable to collectors or other museums. When do you think you'll be able to release the site?"

"No idea. Barney Taylor has been bugging us about that because he wants to get to work on his building project, but that decision isn't up to the police department. I told him to talk to City Hall." She stood up. "Thank you, Nell. You've made my life much easier. I'll pass on this information to the appropriate people and let them wrestle with it, but at least you've cleared up most of the mystery for me."

"Glad to be of service. And I'll admit I learned a lot about Philadelphia and the Revolution just doing the research. I'm glad Harriet passed it on to us, and that we found it at the right time."

"I'll see you out. And I'll let you know if I find anything else that might interest you. People in the city are always digging up historic bits and pieces where they don't expect to."

"I can believe that, if one group managed to mislay four hundred bodies. Please do tell us if you find anything—maybe we could put together an exhibition about unlikely finds."

The detective gave a short bark of laughter. Then I added, "I have one favor to ask."

She cocked an eyebrow. "Yeah?"

"Obviously a discovery like this is going to be big news, at least for a short while. I'd like the Society to get a share of the credit for solving the mystery, if you want to call it that. As you can probably guess, Marty has friends at the newspaper, and she's willing to contact people. Of course the police department would be recognized for their role in this. It should be a good historical interest story."

"I'll clear it with my people, Nell. Besides, nobody would believe that the Philly PD could have solved something like this so fast."

"Thank you, Meredith."

Once outside, I took a deep breath. That meeting had gone well, and I felt we'd scored some points. That was all we'd hoped to do. Now the police and assorted city authorities could take over. I fished out my cell phone and called James.

"Hi, it's me. You busy?"

"Not very. Half the staff is on vacation, and apparently half the criminals."

"Want to have lunch? I just left police HQ and reported what Marty and Dylan and I put together and made the detective a happy woman."

"Sure, but it'll have to be noon—I've got a report to finish," James said.

"Come on over to my place when you're done and we can decide where to go from there."

"Great. See you at noon."

I went back to the Society and reported to Marty and Dylan, who were still chasing down loose ends to the story. They seemed to have formed a bond of sorts, and were happily working together. Dylan was definitely adding to his education this week. Then I left to have lunch with James.

After lunch I was ready to try to drag my attention back to the board report—the meeting was set for Thursday evening—when my phone rang.

"Nell, this is Harold Stevens. Barney Taylor and I have something we'd like to discuss with you. Are you free?"

"Now?"

"That would be convenient, if it's possible."

"Can you come to the Society? We can use the conference room on the ground floor, which should be private. Say, at three?"

"Excellent. We'll be there."

It seemed this story wasn't quite over yet.

Chapter Twenty-one

After I hung up the phone, I tried to figure out why those two wanted to speak with me, much less both of them together. I came up blank, but it had been a busy few days, rewriting a small piece of early American history, and I had other distractions, like the (expletive-deleted) unfinished board report. At least I could clearly demonstrate that I'd been doing my job, and if Detective Hrivnak came through, we'd have some publicity to show for it. I knew that I had learned a lot about local history, and that had given me some new ideas about how to present what we had to the public. I was pretty sure most people—even committed genealogists and serious historians—saw the Society as a nice place filled with dusty old books but kept on walking right past it on their way to sexier sights, like Independence Hall and the Liberty Bell. I doubted we were very high on any tourists' lists, but then, why should a tourist interrupt a tour of one of America's great cities to sit in a library? I wanted to find a way to offer small but memorable doses of what had happened here in the city, and if that meant digging up George Washington's horseshoeing bills, so be it. That conference room on the first floor would be easy to access and was just about the right size for a small, focused exhibit.

I was so busy daydreaming about possibilities that the next time I looked at my watch it was time for my meeting. I gathered my scattered wits and went down to the lobby to greet Barney and Harold, who were waiting for me.

"Gentlemen," I said to them, "I'd say it was lovely to see you again, but it seems like I've just seen you. You want to go sit down and you can tell me what this is about?"

"Please," Harold said stiffly. Barney just looked kind of miserable—maybe his leg hurt.

I led the way to the conference room and shut the door. "So, what's going on? And for heaven's sake, sit down. You look like two kids in the principal's office."

The two men exchanged a glance, then Harold spoke. "We haven't been exactly honest with you, Nell."

"What do you mean by that?" I asked.

Barney answered. "We knew about the other two bodies. And the cannons."

That I hadn't expected to hear. "Before the detective found them?"

"Yes," Barney said. "Right after my crew found the bones from the cemetery."

"And before you told anybody officially?"

"Well, yes. I didn't know what to do. I sent the crew home because I was pretty sure we shouldn't do any more digging right then, but I needed to think. I was kind of wandering around the building lot and I kept stumbling over skulls—it was like a nightmare. And I also knew I couldn't just cover everything up either, because too many people had already seen the bones. So I called Harold."

"Wait—Harold? I thought you called Marty first. Why Harold?"

"My company was one of the contractors for his museum, a few years ago. After that we were drinking buddies, sort of, and I knew he knew something about history. So I asked him to meet me at one of our usual places, and after a couple of beers I told him what I'd found—the cemetery, I mean."

"Uh, Barney, I still don't see the problem here. You called someone in the historical community—that was the right move. Why did you need to call Marty after that, and why didn't you tell her you'd already talked to Harold? And you, Harold—why didn't you mention to Marty that Barney had already talked to you?"

"It's complicated," Harold said glumly.

That was an understatement. "Then somebody had better explain. You asked to see *me* now, right? Not the other way around."

"Nell," Harold began, "I already knew about the other bodies, and the cannons."

"How?"

"I'm Harriet Featherstone's second cousin. Yes, different

surname, but my family passed down the story about how the two men died, and that one was a Featherstone. I assume that Harriet conveyed that information to you somehow."

I nodded. "Yes, she left a detailed letter, which we just found."

Harold went on. "My side of the family never wrote it down. It was kind of a family joke, for years. I didn't have an exact address, but I knew more or less where to look."

"Did the family talk just about the bodies and who they were, or did they mention the cannons too?"

"Both. Without the cannons there would have been no bodies. Look, I don't know if anyone in the family actually believed the whole thing, but it made for good conversation. Before you ask, I never went looking for them until now."

"So why didn't you just tell somebody?" I was getting close to exploding.

Now Harold and Barney were avoiding looking at each other. "Well," Barney began, "I was running kind of short of money for the project already, and Harold suddenly got interested. He said something like, 'I know how we can make some money fast, but you're going to have to help me, and you can't talk about it to anyone else.' Then he told me that family story, about the bodies and the cannons. We were already kind of drunk, so we decided to see if it was true, and went back to the site. Harold knew where to look, and we found 'em."

Very little of this was making sense to me. "And I'll say again— why didn't you just report this to someone then?"

"Ask Harold," Barney said.

I turned to Harold. "Talk," I demanded.

"Nell, do you have any idea how much pristine eighteenth-century cannons dating from the Revolution will bring at auction or sale?"

"Of course I don't," I snapped. "I deal with books."

"Conservatively, twenty-five to fifty thousand dollars apiece. To both museums and private buyers. From a quick glance, it looked like we had a couple of dozen. Conservatively the lot would be worth maybe seven hundred and fifty thousand dollars."

"Honestly? Or on the black market?" I had no idea if there was a black market for cannons, but these two guys were acting pretty strange about the whole thing.

Harold just shrugged without answering. "So there we were, with a load of cannons that nobody else knew about. And Barney had machines on the lot across the street that would be capable of moving them. All we needed was a truck for transport, and we'd be on our way. We'd hide them, then I'd sell them, and we'd split the proceeds."

"So what went wrong? Because clearly something did."

"Coming out of the bar I tripped and tore up my ankle," Barney said. "Which meant I couldn't handle the heavy machinery, and we didn't dare bring anyone else into the deal. But we thought we could wait for a day or two. We didn't know that Marty had seen a body all those years ago and would go looking for it again."

"So you called her about the cemetery bodies not knowing that she knew about the other one, and then the police discovered us poking around, and everything snowballed. And of course Marty thought of Harold first when we discovered the cannons on our own and called him."

"Yes. And our whole plan went up in smoke. Too many people knew too much."

"So we foiled your devious scheme. That was when you disappeared from the lot?"

"Yes. My leg was killing me, even though I had it wrapped up, so I figured I'd better get it looked at, and you know how long waiting time is in the ER around here, so I didn't manage to get back to the lot. And they X-rayed the leg and taped it up again and gave me some really great painkillers, and I went home and crashed."

That made some sort of sense. "Tell me, Harold—do you have any idea whose property those cannons would be now, after all these years? We know who lived in that building when they were hidden, but after that? Do they belong to the descendants of the family? To the city? Would your museum make a play for them? And why the hell are you telling me this now? I probably would never have known."

"When we knew our plan was dead, I decided that we'd better get on the right side of the story. Much the way you no doubt plan to, Nell," Harold said. "Our establishments need the publicity, crass though that sounds."

I sat back in my seat and stared at them. They'd been planning a major crime, although I wasn't sure who would have suffered. But it still had to be a crime, until proven otherwise. But for various reasons the plan had collapsed, and now they were coming clean, but only to me. What was my responsibility here? I wished I could ask James, but that would have to wait.

"So what do you want out of this?" I asked Harold.

"I think we should collaborate on getting the story out. You know the history and the people involved, and I've got information on the cannons and their history. It's a win-win situation for both of us."

He had a point, I had to concede. Instead of stealing valuable historic artifacts, he might even come out looking like a hero, or at least an expert. "My name—and the Society's—comes first on any public discussion. After all, Marty and I were made aware of the bodies and the cannons legitimately. But I think we can work together. While you might have been planning an illegal act, it never happened, and no one could prove otherwise."

"What about me?" Barney said plaintively.

I wanted to tell the man that the publicity would be good for his project, but I still wondered if people would be uncomfortable living on a former cemetery site, and would they feel sure that all the bodies were gone? "Maybe you can work out some sort of finder's fee with the city. Don't give up hope just yet—at least your building will be famous."

Barney brightened, but only a bit.

"You won't share this information with anyone, will you, Nell?" Harold asked anxiously.

"I'll let you decide how much you want to tell publicly. From the Society's end the story stands on its own merits." I stood up. "I've got to start working on the publicity. This story should have a lot of popular appeal, and I want to catch the next news cycle. But thank you for filling me in."

"It seemed right that you should know, Nell," Harold told me. "We are, after all, colleagues."

Of a sort, I admitted to myself, but I wasn't quite ready to trust him. "I appreciate your telling me. I'll see you out."

Chapter Twenty-two

I managed to cobble together the board report in record time. The accuracy of its details might be questionable, but at least the Society wasn't losing money—no easy feat in these days when there were so many demands for funding for a wide range of municipal and private projects. I also happened to know that most board members couldn't be bothered to read all the details of my careful spreadsheets, choosing instead to go straight to the bottom line. Only a couple ever asked me later about one point or another. Frankly, like many cultural institutions, board members were chosen for their ability to contribute significant money, and those who accepted the "honor" did it for the prestige, whether or not they ever showed up for meetings or events, not because they cared deeply for history or documents or the city of Philadelphia. But the system worked, and I wasn't about to change things.

But at tonight's meeting I had a surprise for the board. I'd asked Marty to attend, to back me up—while she was no longer a board member, most of the current members knew her well and weren't about to object. Dylan was tucked in a corner, listening eagerly.

I cleared my throat and began. "Ladies and gentlemen, while this is a regularly scheduled board meeting, I have some interesting news to present to you. The summary of the Society's financial position is in front of you, and you may go home and study it on your own, but the bottom line is that we're in good shape, or as good as any cultural institution in the city. But what I need to describe to you is both an interesting piece of the city's history, and a significant opportunity for the Society to extend its reach within the community as well as collaborate with one of our fellow institutions in a new and unusual way."

Almost everyone seemed to be paying attention, while a few looked at their watches—they were used to short meetings. "You may have noticed some small news items in the paper or online over the past few days, involving a construction project only a few blocks away. I won't go into the details, and most have not been released publicly yet, but it promises to be a significant archeological find. This past weekend a cemetery which has been forgotten and paved over for more than a century was uncovered by a local contractor. Its discovery in turn led to another discovery, smaller but more significant." I proceeded to give an abbreviated report on what Marty and Dylan and I had uncovered over the past few days. I segued into Harold Stevens's role. I tried to keep it short and to the point, but I wanted to convey the importance of what we had learned and how we could take advantage of that on behalf of the Society.

"What I'm proposing now is that the Society and the new Revolutionary War museum work together to interpret what we found. The Society has the documentary resources, while the museum has the expertise in historic artifacts and, in particular, armaments. This collaborative effort will enhance the visibility of both institutions, and will offer a new way of looking at local history. I would like the Society to spearhead this effort, since we have already done the basic research, and we are working with the city to fill in some of the blanks."

"What will it cost us?" someone from the other end of the table demanded.

"Very little, in fact. As I said, we've already done much of the basic research, and we wouldn't be involved in any physical excavation. What I'm asking of you, the board, is to approve the staff's efforts to serve as the public interpreter of the archeological evidence as it emerges, and to make our findings an effective teaching tool, drawing together the resources of multiple organizations within the city. We have the staff and the documentation at our disposal, but I'd like to see you support it with enthusiasm. You don't have to vote today, if you choose not to, but the news is going to go viral very quickly, and I want us to take the lead."

"Nothing like a pile of old bones to get people's attention," another member commented.

165

"That's very true—particularly when there are over four hundred corpses. Yes, it's a ghoulish fascination, but in this case it's reality, and what happened in that neighborhood is a page of the city's history, in more ways than one."

The board chair, Lewis Howard, who had remained silent so far, spoke for the first time. "I suggest that we give our staff, including our president, the opportunity to engage in an exploratory phase of this investigation. If it pans out in, say, a couple of months, then we can authorize a fuller exploration. If necessary we can call a special meeting of the board. But as it stands, as of this moment, Ms. Pratt has presented us with an extraordinary opportunity, and we would be ignoring the Society's fundamental mission if we failed to take advantage of it."

"Thank you, Lewis. Do you wish to take a vote now?" I figured I might as well strike while the iron was hot.

The vote passed unanimously. We were adding bodies and cannons to the Society's repertory.

The board meeting dissolved very quickly after that, but we'd given everyone something to think about, and I was encouraged by their initial reaction. I looked around at my partners in research. "Marty, Dylan, we have just changed a small piece of history. I vote we go out and celebrate."

Marty smiled. "I second that motion."

"All in favor?"

The vote was unanimous.

Postscript

I worked as a fund-raiser at the Historical Society of Pennsylvania—the model for Nell Pratt's Society for the Preservation of Pennsylvania Antiquities in this series—for several years, and I was familiar with the parts of the city near the Delaware River (such as Second Street, which plays an important part in this story). Therefore I was surprised when I was doing some research on more recent events in Philadelphia (it's been a while since I worked there) to read about the discovery of a long-abandoned cemetery in a part of town I thought I knew—and that it took place in 2017. I knew I had to make it a central part of this book.

That cemetery was closed in 1860, and it seems incredible that it was lost for so long, doesn't it? And yes, there were over four hundred bodies left behind, under the paving. The discovery was widely covered in local news at the time. What's more, it's only one of the abandoned cemeteries in the city. And yes, the Historical Society does have a copy of the list of bodies buried in the lost cemetery.

But I also used some creative liberty by adding another discovery under an old building across the street from the site of that cemetery. That part of the story was inspired by Washington's crossing the Delaware River on Christmas 1776 in order to attack the British forces at Trenton. It's one of those stories that captures the imagination of schoolchildren, aided by the iconic image painted by Emanuel Leutze of Washington standing in a small boat as he and some of his men crossed the river, but it was a bit more complicated than just getting to the other side. There were thousands of American soldiers who made that crossing in small boats in a raging blizzard, surrounded by ice floes (and a lot of them were late to arrive)—and won the battle.

The mythology of the smugglers' tunnels leading from the waterfront also survives today.

Philadelphia is a surprising mix of historic and modern elements, and it's a pleasure to write about it. The Society (under whichever name) is an outstanding repository of historic research materials, and one of the best genealogy libraries in the country—well worth a visit if you're putting together your family tree. And it seems there's always something new to be found, even after centuries.

About the Author

After collecting too many degrees and exploring careers ranging from art historian to investment banker to professional genealogist, Sheila Connolly began writing mysteries in 2001 and is now a full-time writer.

She wrote her first mystery series for Berkley Prime Crime under the name Sarah Atwell, and the first book, *Through a Glass, Deadly*, was nominated for an Agatha Award for Best First Novel.

Under her own name, her Orchard Mystery Series debuted with *One Bad Apple* and has been followed by twelve more books in the series.

Her Museum Mysteries, set in the Philadelphia museum community, opened with *Fundraising the Dead* and continued with eight more books.

Her County Cork Mysteries debuted with *Buried in a Bog*, followed by six more novels.

She has also published numerous original ebooks with Beyond the Page: *Sour Apples, Once She Knew, The Rising of the Moon, Reunion with Death, Under the Hill, Relatively Dead, Seeing the Dead, Defending the Dead, Watch for the Dead, Search for the Dead,* and *Revealing the Dead*.

Sheila is a member of Sisters in Crime, Mystery Writers of America, and Romance Writers of America. She is a former President of Sisters in Crime New England, and was cochair for the 2011 New England Crime Bake conference.

Made in the USA
Las Vegas, NV
09 February 2022

43517540R00104